"Don't look so startled," Matt laughed softly. "I'm not going to push you into anything until you are ready. I want you to share my vision, Bliss. If you feel as I do?"

He pulled her gently back to him. *Oh, yes, Matt, yes,* her heart cried out. But her logical mind said something quite different. *No, no, it can never be!*

With a little cry of despair born of a broken heart, Bliss pushed against Matt's chest. "It's all a dream —a cruel joke!" she struggled to hold back the sobs that rose to her throat. "We've hardly met—and you *couldn't* be interested in—in me—"

Grabbing her wrists, Matt held them so tightly she felt her fingers tingle for want of blood. "*Interested!*" he spat the word out furiously. "Why not? Just tell me why not."

JUNE MASTERS BACHER is a highly gifted author who not only shares her talents in *Guideposts*, but also delights her audience with pioneer romance novels such as *Love Is A Gentle Stranger*, *Love's Silent Song*, and *Diary of a Loving Heart*. More recently she combines her storytelling with mysterious twists in Christian romance novels, including *The Heart That Lingers*, *Until There Was You*, and *With All My Heart*.

Aharon Chupp

When Love Shines Through

BY

June Masters Bacher

HARVEST HOUSE PUBLISHERS
Eugene, Oregon 97402

WHEN LOVE SHINES THROUGH

Copyright © 1984 Harvest House Publishers
Eugene, Oregon 97402

ISBN 0-89081-430-9

Printed in the United States of America.

Dedicated
to
my Family of Cousins,
who are closer "kin" to me!

There is nothing holier in this life of ours than the first consciousness of love—the first fluttering of its silken wings—the first rising sound and breath of that wind which is so soon to sweep through the soul, to purify or to destroy.

—LONGFELLOW

Chapter One

"*L*ast call. Flight 107, nonstop to New York!"
Bliss McVay shook her head in disbelief,
the protective curtain of her long, straw-
colored hair parting to reveal her disfigured face.
For once she did not care.

"No romance can end this way," she murmured tonelessly. *No, not even an imagined
one... my plane! I must hurry...*

The beautiful daydream had come more and
more frequently of late. Undoubtedly, psychol-
ogists would say it was because she was retreat-
ing further into her private world. But Bliss had
held onto it tenaciously. After all, it was *her*
fantasy—not some stranger's. And one day it

would come true. It *had* to! Otherwise, the conflicting nightmare might become a reality. That
thought was too horrible, too real to accept. So
she drifted deeper into the daydream.

Always it was the same. She stood atop a hill,
so high it probed the sky, her filmy white dress
billowed out by a little breeze. The Cloud
Princess, that's what she was, waiting for her
Prince. The breeze moved to ruffle her hair with
gentle fingers, then swept it playfully from her
face. But it no longer mattered, for the disfigur-
ing, purple birthmark which had once covered
the right side of her face was gone. The once-
muddy skin had changed, too. It was now a polished ivory and her eyes sparkled with a never-
before light. All was silent around her except for
the pounding she knew was her heart. And then
the pounding grew louder... *louder*...
LOUDER... until she knew the familiar sound
of hoofbeats had joined her heart's wild cadence.

And then he was there! Her knight in shining
armor! Up, up, up he rode on a magnificent
steed whose nostrils flanged with the agony of
speed as horse and rider ascended the winding
trail. Soon, very soon she would be swept into
the silver saddle and they would gallop away—
perhaps to another galaxy.

Bliss could never bring herself to look up and
see the man's face. But there was no need. It
was Jason Blackwell, of course. Only the darkly-

beautiful man was no longer her employer. He was her True Love, the core of her Impossible Dream...

But today the dream had exploded, leaving no spark of hope. Just ashes. Ashes of a dead love. Ashes of her last hope. Ashes—she could taste their arid bitterness in her mouth.

• • •

The day had begun like all other days. The usual hurried shower, skimpy breakfast, and rush to get ahead of the heavy traffic across the Bay Bridge and to the high-rise office, housing the home office of Blackwell and Son's Interior Decorating firm. There had been no time to read the morning mail. Not that it mattered. Ads, bills, maybe a note from Mother postmarked Chicago where she had taken an apartment to be near Miriam. Bliss knew the words by heart. Miriam was *so* beautiful...her husband *so* successful...the twins *so* bright...oh, how she wished Bliss would "come out of that shell" and make something of herself. Bliss sighed. It was no secret that her younger sister was her mother's favorite. "My swan," Mother said of Miriam's pale coloring, her willowy grace.

"Which makes me the 'ugly duckling,' " Bliss had replied once. Her mother did not dispute it.

"You're like your father's side. They were all—well, gangly—but goodness only knows where the unsightly birthmark came from!"

Bliss had cringed, let her hair grow to hang unbecomingly about her face as a shield, and eventually slumped forward to break her height. But the greatest change was inside. Bliss resigned herself that she would never be one of the lucky ones, someone whose Mr. Right came along. There was nothing she would like better than a clean house smelling of freshly-baked bread. But girls like her didn't stand a chance. Only the beautiful ones won the trophies.

And then, when she was desperately lonely after a long unfulfilling day's work as file clerk at Blackwell Interiors, the daydreams began. Or was it the first time she set eyes on Jason? He had not so much as looked her direction when he reviewed her resume and asked a few questions when she applied for the position as his secretary. Rumor had it that he was looking for efficiency and that the young man did not mix business with pleasure. Well, that was fine. Certainly, she was efficient, what with all her working experience and high scholastic record. Not every girl was valedictorian of her high school's graduating class. Yes, it was fine that the younger Mr. Blackwell didn't mind her being bright. Fine, too, that he would not be thrusting his attentions upon her. Fine—until she met him!

But when Bliss looked up into Jason Blackwell's darkly-beautiful face, it was not fine at all.

Italian, wasn't he, with that abundant black hair, olive skin, and the impenetrable dark eyes? The fact that the handsome mouth was set in a hard line did not bother her. Sorrow, perhaps. Maybe disappointment at not having met a girl with a warm and loving heart. At any rate, Jason was the object of her dreams. Her reason for being alive. One day he would see beyond the exterior of herself. . .discover her. . .and. . .

All these thoughts Bliss was reviewing as she negotiated the last turn leading to the building where she worked, handed the car key to the attendant, and hurried to the gold-lettered office which only she could enter. Her office joined that of Jason's private quarters which she entered only by invitation except in the early morning. He arrived an hour after she came in at nine, giving her time to check that everything was in order. Not a part of her job, but she loved doing it—down to the last detail, even seeing that fresh flowers were on his desk. She expected no thank-yous.

It was not until she was standing in the little hallway which joined the rooms together that she realized Jason was there. And that he was not alone. She heard a low feminine laugh—familiar, but hard to place. Hesitating so as to make no noise as she retreated, Bliss placed her hand on the doorknob as quietly as possible. It was then that she heard the fatal words.

"You are so beautiful—so beautiful, my love," Jason was saying huskily. "Truly, all homely girls should be drowned at birth! Take my secretary—"

But Bliss heard no more. The daydream faded. And the nightmare came . . .

Without waiting for the dark hours of night, it came. The same setting and plot, a great field of wind-bent poppies—lovely, oh, so lovely, their vibrant oranges and yellows speaking of the fire that burned within her heart. And she, as erect and beautiful as in the daydream, rode her lover's white steed and rushed eagerly to a secret rendezvous. With outstretched arms, he appeared from the misty nowhere . . . reaching for her, reaching . . . only to drop his arms, let out a mocking laugh, and turn back to the mists from which he emerged. She was rejected, scorned —but *why*? And then she knew. The terrible birthmark was back. She was once more the ugly duckling, the unnoticed fixture in his office. Her head dropped in shame, letting the horse's white mane and her long hair, once again colorless, cover her face from the hateful world of reality . . .

Only this time it was true. Just as she had known it would be someday. Without thinking further, Bliss had rushed to her office, grabbed her bag and light wrap, and made her way blindly to the elevator. She would go home, call in sick—for sick she was, sick in a way that no anti-biotic could heal.

When she arrived at her small apartment, she found the telegram . . . and here she was aboard a 747 heading for New York. It was all a dream, this trip and how it had come about. But neither daydream nor nightmare—just unreal. Things like this did not happen in real life.

Who would have supposed that such a common, ordinary-looking—correction, she wasn't even ordinary, but a *freak*—would be chosen for the complete beauty makeover sponsored by *Tomorrow*, one of the big city's leading fashion magazines? Certainly, she had entertained no hope of winning when she filled in the blanks: NAME, Bliss McVay; AGE, 25; HEIGHT, 5'8"; WEIGHT, 110; COLORING, muddy skin, sun-bleached hair, and tortoise-shell eyes, she wrote. She had grinned at the description.

The photograph Bliss included was a copy of her identification card for entering the Blackwell Building, a side view. The photographer, she remembered, had been difficult. The pictures had to be full-face. That was out, she said—even if it meant her job. Pretty risky, she knew even then, as she had been only a file clerk, her good mind still "undiscovered." But she had won out, a triumph which had paid off later. If Jason had seen a front view or—perish the thought!—a view of the right side of her face, he would never have granted the interview three years later which led to her job as his secretary.

With that thought, the pain came again—a knife plunged into her heart but not withdrawn so that death could come quickly. No, the lethal object was left intact, allowing the blood to ooze out drop by drop so that what remained of her life would be a living death.

Only it wouldn't be! It was Jason who would suffer. Transformed, she would entice him, lead him on, then cast him aside. . . if only she had the strength, which in weak moments she doubted. Mrs. Bronson, who owned the apartment house where Bliss had a bright, sunny corner overlooking the Pacific, had vowed that the telegram was an "answer to prayer." She claimed only the Lord could bring about such miracles. Bliss had neither contradicted nor agreed with the motherly woman. Why talk about matters about which she knew nothing? But now as she took her seat on the plane, she found herself wishing there were some higher power—the Good Fairy, maybe—whom she could ask for strength to go through with this plan. . .

So buried in thought and conflicting emotions was she that Bliss did not look up to see a tall, casually-dressed young man making his way toward her. She was vaguely aware of a stir of excitement and then a hush as, seeing that his seat assignment number matched her own, he paused by her side.

"Pardon me, miss, but we seem to be sharing the same seat!"

The voice was rich and low. It also held a touch of humor. . . humor she had no time for.

"I don't think so," she said, keeping her face carefully turned toward the window by which she sat.

The person to whom the voice belonged busied himself putting his carry-on luggage in the compartment above her head. *Well, let him! He can have the fun of unloading it when one of the plane's attendants comes by.*

Until then, she would ignore the man. Only that was impossible. He was addressing her and Bliss did not intend being rude; but she had no intention of giving up her seat either. It was a part of her shield, a way to keep her disfigured face from prying faces which seemed to see behind the sunglasses and dark veil she wore.

"Would you mind very much—" the voice began again and then hesitated almost shyly. "Look, I am as embarrassed about this as you are—but I *am* assigned to the seat you occupy. If I could see your assignment. I mean—would you mind?"

At least he had the grace not to sit down, Bliss thought as she fished in her bag. Handing him the card, she turned farther to the right.

"I see," he said quietly. "This should have been your seat. But if you prefer the one by the window—"

"Oh, please, yes!" Her words were almost a cry.

Bliss felt the man's eyes on her as he eased an obviously long frame into the seat next to the aisle. But he had the good sense not to try to engage her in what would have been an unwelcome conversation.

Takeoff was smooth. The big plane leveled off at a high elevation and Bliss found herself looking down upon a cumulus-cloud world. The perfect setting for the daydream. Only it was gone forever. Like Jason's love. Now there was only the nightmare. And revenge.

What seemed like hours of silence later, except for the hum of the engines, Bliss was aware that someone was speaking to her. "Lunch, miss," her seatmate said softly.

In a reflex action, she pulled down the shelf in front of her, keeping her face carefully averted. Surely, she should thank the man. He had been kind.

"Thank you," she murmured. "I'm afraid I have been ungracious—and certainly poor company."

He took her tray before answering. "I've done nothing to help, I'm afraid. And where does it say that young ladies are expected to make conversation with strangers who try to take their seats?"

Bliss felt the beginnings of a smile. There was something comforting about this man's presence. How long had it been since a man other than Jason had stirred any feeling within her? But here she was, high above the earth leaving one shattered world and entering a strange one—and in need of a friend. It must be the craziness of the day . . . or the high altitude . . . but suddenly she thought, *I need someone to lean on.* Maybe this man beside her would be that someone.

"The London broil is delicious," he encouraged softly, somehow managing to make the words sound as if she need not answer unless she wished. Then she realized she had not touched her food. And suddenly she was hungry, what with an abbreviated breakfast and the trials of the day.

And admittedly, someone caring enough about her to encourage eating—even a stranger—came at a good time. Had anybody ever cared? *Really* cared about her? Maybe if her parents had stayed together . . . but they had separated before Bliss had any clear memory of her father and Mother had eyes only for Miriam. Because other children teased about the birthmark, she shied away from them and dug deeper and deeper into her studies.

But if somebody cared enough now—automatically, Bliss reached for her fork and then laid it down. There was no way to get a forkful of food behind the veil.

"I'm not really hungry," she murmured.

"Wouldn't it help if you removed the—uh, hat, scarf, what *do* they call those things?"

"Veils." The word was almost inaudible.

The throbbing in her chest was suffocating. All the pain, loneliness, and disillusionment of childhood and her recent humiliation were back, tormenting and taunting. This faceless man would be no different. She had no right to expect him to be. What did she have to offer? Maybe Jason was right, after all. A hot tear spilled down her cheek and splashed onto her hand. Better she was dead. . .

Once again the stranger beside her spoke. "I must apologize! I am so sorry if I have offended you in some way. You see, I had no idea that perhaps the veil was a symbol of your faith—"

"Faith!" Bliss had not meant the word to come out so harshly. Embarrassed, she lowered her voice to its normal, whispery pitch. "It's more an indication that I have no faith at all."

The man seemed taken aback. "You mean—you can't mean—something to do with the occult?" There was a plea in the low-pitched voice.

It was Bliss's turn to be shocked. Oh, how did

she get into this conversation?

Horrified, she could only whisper, "Devil worship? Oh, no! Not that! Never in a million years."

She was about to say that she knew nothing of God either, but there was no time.

He exhaled in obvious relief. "I'm so glad," he interrupted as if it were important what she thought one way or another.

Who was this strange man anyway? Maybe there would be an opportunity to steal a glance at him soon, because suddenly it was imperative that he have a face.

Maybe if I make it clear that I want to be left alone, Bliss thought, *he will decide to rest.* Then she would dare look his direction—

But he was speaking again.

"Somehow I can't think of your donning that veil in celebration of a divorce—"

Bliss realized later that she spoke too hastily.

"Oh no! Not that either! I've never been married—I'm not even—" Then because she was angry at herself for saying more than he had asked, she added bluntly, "Has bereavement occurred to you?"

Again, the quick intake of breath.

"Again, I must apologize, my dear. I have done and said all the wrong things. And no, I never thought of your being in mourning. Please accept my apology—*and* my condolences."

Mutely, Bliss nodded. *It's true,* she thought

desperately. *I am indeed in mourning. Someone has passed out of my life, yes, but it is I who has died.*

The stewardess picked up the trays. Bliss snapped the shelf shut and turned as far away as possible, closing her eyes as if to rest.

When someone touched her hand, she jumped. Jerking her head erect, she almost— but, thankfully, not quite—turned to face the intruder. Quickly, she turned away, aware that the touch had come from the man beside her.

"I just wanted to assure you that I was not attempting a pickup."

"I never thought that," Bliss said truthfully.

"And I had no right to pry."

"I never thought that either."

"I sensed that you were troubled—"

He paused as if waiting for her to confirm or deny. When she said nothing, he sighed. "I can see that I made a nuisance of myself—and in your time of trouble."

No, no! It isn't like that either! But before there was a chance to put the denial into words, Bliss sensed that he was turning away.

The plane hit a wind pocket. The pilot apologized for the turbulence. They climbed to a higher elevation and there was calm.

Bliss opened her eyes to the great puffer-belly clouds below, pillared and domed like castles. But she was no longer the Cloud Princess.

"That's what I'm mourning—the death of a dream!"

The man beside her did not stir. Neither did he sound surprised.

"Dreams die hard," he said gently. And then he added, "It is better that we see visions, leaving dreams to old men. Isn't that the way the Scripture goes?"

"I don't know," Bliss answered meekly.

And this time he fell silent.

What seemed a long time later to Bliss, she turned her head gradually toward her seatmate. He had been so silent and so still that she felt he might be sleeping. She couldn't be sure. But at least his eyes were closed.

Quickly she scanned his face and what she saw quickened her pulse and conversely made her sick at heart.

Small wonder there had been a stir of excitement when he came in. Here, sitting beside her, was the most incredibly handsome young man she had ever seen.

His face had a sculptured look like the Greek gods she had seen chiseled in the art museums. There was a blonde sheen about the look—the kind seen in photographs.

Perfect! Perfect in every way.

Well, what had she expected? Another loser like herself? An object of ridicule?

No . . . not that . . . a possible friend. And this

man, this proud and beautiful man, could never be friends with such as her.

It didn't matter. It didn't matter at all!

Oh, yes, it did. It mattered very much. Too much, as a matter of fact.

She turned away to hide the tears.

Chapter Two

The man beside her seemed lost in his own thoughts. When at length he spoke, Bliss jumped.

"Sorry, I didn't mean to bump you."

"You didn't," Bliss assured him.

"I think both my legs are asleep," he laughed. "Isn't it time for a seventh-inning stretch?"

It was indeed. Bliss had sat cramped in the one position, her neck twisted far to the right, for so long that every muscle ached and every nerve ending tingled.

When the long, tweedy legs swung into the aisle, Bliss dared to turn from the window. Then, pulling her weight across the chair adjoining hers, she quickly turned the opposite direction. Carefully avoiding the eyes of other passengers, she made her way to the "First Class" section.

A stewardess was serving cocktails. "Problem, miss?" she asked significantly.

"No—I—" Bliss beat a hasty retreat, hoping to get there before her handsome seatmate. It occurred to her suddenly that she did not even know his name. Not that it mattered.

She was first to arrive. And then the impossible happened. In her haste to be seated before the man returned, Bliss tripped over her small carry-on bag, dumping the entire contents of her handbag onto the floor. At that moment, the plane chose to tilt crazily sending her billfold sliding beneath her chair, her lipstick rolling down the aisle, and all the correspondence between her and *Tomorrow* magazine flying the entire length of the aisle.

Frantically, she bent to recover whatever she could. The lipstick, of course, she was unable to reach. Forget that. Her lips were invisible behind the veil, hopefully. But she must find her billfold, her plane ticket, and all the identifying papers the magazine editor had sent. She was scratching wildly at the elusive belongings which kept rolling just beyond reach when she was aware suddenly of a head bent intimately to her own.

"You!" she gasped.

"Am I that awful?"

Reaching to capture the elusive lipstick case, the man she had practically crossed the continent with let his tanned, long-fingered hand rest briefly on her own pale one.

You aren't awful at all. You are perfect. Just perfect. And that is what is wrong. The thought made her want to cry.

"It was clumsy of me—" she murmured.

The man was fishing beneath his own seat to get her billfold. When he pulled it out, Bliss saw to her horror that everything had fallen from it, too.

"It's all here, I think," he said, turning his face to one side in order to reach farther. And piece by piece he handed her the contents.

"I don't know how to thank you," Bliss said softly. "I—I'm afraid I've been pretty terrible—"

And without thinking it through, she reached out her hand to him. What happened next was a nightmare. Somehow her fingers became entwined in the veil and the small pillbox hat holding it in place fell to the floor. Her face, turned toward the beautiful stranger, was exposed in all its ugliness. Hat, veil, and glasses gone!

She let out a gasp of horror and then collapsed in weak tears. Only a few more hours and he would have never known. She could have been spared one last embarrassment. If ever they met again—unlikely!—she would be beautiful.

"There, there," the nice voice was saying, as warm, strong arms eased her into her seat. Without their strength, Bliss knew that she would never have made it without fainting. No food. The awfulness of the day. And now this!

"Now you see. Now you know—know the secret of the lady in the long, dark veil." Sobs choked out the last words.

His arms tightened around her. "I only see a sad and lonely girl—a girl whom life has hurt so much—a girl I want to comfort and don't know how.

"You mean you can bear to look at me—still want me for a friend?" She was drowning in tears.

He seemed genuinely surprised, Bliss realized as she let him mop her face with a large, white handkerchief that smelled of the outdoors. "Tell me," he teased, "just what do you think little boys are made of?"

" 'Rags and tags and old paper bags,' " she sputtered through tears and the beginnings of a laugh. "That's what my grandmother used to say."

"Tell me about her. My name is Matthew, most call me Matt—and now about your grandmother?"

"I don't remember her very well," Bliss said obediently. "I mostly remember an old, rambling house—haunted, she told us—with all sorts of secret places and a range of sounds, made by 'other presences,' she said. I fantasized along with her. Maybe I even believed them. Then the sense of wonder faded—and I stopped believing. Oh, Matthew—Matt—why did I stop believing?"

Matt was silent for a moment and then he said, " 'When I was a child, I spake as a child, I understood as a child, I thought as a child; but when I became a man, I put away childish things.' "

"I've heard that somewhere," Bliss said slowly.

"First Corinthians 13:11," he said matter-of-factly. "Did your grandmother tell you Bible stories?"

"No, I don't think so—no, she never did, and neither did my parents. But my grandmother took me to a church once. I remember cherubs leaning down from the wall so close I could almost touch them. I begged her to take me back, but she never did. Even then, I was interested in interior decorating."

Matt shifted down comfortably in his seat. "Is that what you do?"

Bliss felt flustered. She hadn't intended getting into anything personal. "Sort of," she answered vaguely. Then, before there were further questions, she returned to the subject of her grandmother's home. "It was a big white, clapboard house that sort of shimmered, I remember

—and it was surrounded by a forest of gnarled trees. And, oh, the house had eyes! All those windows I never did get around to counting seemed to be watching from the three-story building—even in the dark." Involuntarily, she trembled.

"It *sounds* haunted," Matt laughed.

"Maybe it was." Bliss felt Matt's questioning eyes on her. "Well, no, but I do have mixed feelings about those fragments of memory. Sometimes I think what a wonderful place to raise a family—attics, cellars, and all those porches. Still," she hesitated, "it's probably where all the dreams started."

"Tell me about them."

"Oh, no! I couldn't possibly." Aghast at having mentioned the subject which she had never spoken of before, and most assuredly not to a stranger, Bliss felt her heart turn over. And certainly she should not have mentioned a family!

"Dreams are just that. No more. No less." His positive tone was reassuring. "Like I told you, we can turn them into visions if we try. Say," he leaned toward her slightly, "I don't even know your name—and we're having such a good time. I don't want to say 'Hey, you!' "

When he leaned back into his former position, it seemed safe to answer. He was right. They were having a nice talk. What harm could there be in sharing her name?

"My name is Bliss."

Did she imagine his quick intake of breath? "What a lovely name!" There could be no mistaking the admiration in his words. "And it is right for you. It goes with the beautiful, whispery voice. Why, you have *me* half-believing in your fantasies."

Something happened to Bliss's senses then. Something heady. As if she had been inhaling too many roses after a spring rain. And something happened to her heart. It wanted to burst —the way she felt when she heard a first robin or watched the blue of the night meet the gold of the day along the margin of San Francisco Bay.

Did this stranger realize that he was the first man in her life to pay her a compliment?

"Tell me more about your dreams, the ones brought on by the old house," this man called Matt coaxed.

She should be blushing from his praise. She should be stuttering the way she always did when speaking with a stranger . . . faltering . . . doing the wrong things. Instead, she felt giddy with a strange euphoria, born perhaps from the lack of food and the unexpected praise, however small.

"Oh, the dreams," she said, her voice sounding other-worldly in her own ears. "Actually, there were two of them—"

And suddenly she, Bliss McVay, the ugly duckling who trusted nobody and believed in nothing, was telling about the daydream and the nightmare to a stranger . . .

Chapter Three

“Bliss found herself caught up in a dream world of sudden serenity. The plane seat became a hammock in which she rocked to and fro, nestled as she was between rolling hills of cumulus clouds rising like dormant volcanos from a turquoise sea of sky.

A part of her talked with the man beside her, who had become a part of the high-altitude dream. Another part tried to rear its ugly head. “Remember your mission...be cautious.... don't be caught up in this web again...it's a fantasy like those of childhood...”

But the dream world won out. When Matt asked why she had left the old house, Bliss replied, "I guess a part of me never did. It was only the dreams that died—they always do, you know—" She paused when she became aware that bitterness had crept into her voice.

Why *had* she left? The house went for unpaid taxes. A shame. Nobody in the family wanted it. Except Bliss. No, not even her, she thought quickly. She had run away as fast as her little legs could carry her on that last visit. Why? Because fear, like a cold vise, had closed around her childish heart.

"There are things in this life we can't understand or explain, my child," her grandmother had said. "But that doesn't mean they don't exist—"

And before the strange, old lady could finish speaking, her granddaughter had fled into the elfin forest. Fled lest she, too, become "peculiar." That's what the townspeople called her grandmother—peculiar—only maybe she had waited too long. *Some* force had caused the horrible birthmark.

Bliss suddenly needed reassurance from the man beside her. With new boldness, she turned and looked again at the perfect profile. No, not quite perfect. It seemed to give her a certain sense of satisfaction to see a scar tracing his profile, beginning at the forehead and running the length of the sculptured face—pinching the beautiful mouth. Odd, she hadn't noticed it before.

She strained her eyes to see in the gathering twilight. But shadows were playing on the ceiling of the cabin—shifting, changing, charged with new energy when her eyes met his. But the eyes were changed, too. They glowed with a look of strain.

There was no scar! Matt was in pain.

Surprised at her own concern, Bliss leaned forward. "What is it, Matt? What is wrong?"

For a moment, he turned away from her. She was glad when he turned back. "Nothing you should worry about. A game leg."

But his tone was unconvincing. "Recent?" Bliss asked, wondering if he were an athlete.

"Yes—and no. The injury happened some time ago on the set, but the complications came later—"

Maybe Matthew said more. Later, Bliss was to regret that she had not listened. But her ears had stopped functioning with his use of "on the set." Wasn't that movie and television talk?

Without thinking, Bliss did something which was totally out of character. "Are you an actor?"

He sighed and seemed to hesitate. " '*Was*' is the better word," he said slowly. "Not a star, mind you, just a man with a vision—until this."

An actor. She was seated beside an actor. Bliss wondered why she had not panicked. Here she was carrying on a conversation with a celebrity when a few words were all she could manage with everyday people in her life.

This man was accustomed to glamorous actresses, spanning the spectrum from leggy chorus girls to statuesque beauties named for Oscar nominations. But the thought did not shatter her. Instead, she felt the grave concern one reserves for a near and dear friend—or someone closer—when there is pain.

"Tell me about it," Bliss whispered.

"Which part?"

"All of it," Bliss heard herself saying.

And then their dinner came. As Matt talked, Bliss ate what was undoubtedly a simple meal as if she were dining at some banquet hall. She was hungry, but there was more. This was the first time in her life that a man—and certainly not someone as important as Matthew—had ever talked with her. *Really* talked. In a way that makes a vision come alive.

And so she dined on tiny sandwiches of creamed cheese and exotic smoked salmon, crabmeat, aspics, and avocados vinaigrette. Did she imagine it or did Matt really cut some kind of steak in wine sauce into miniscule pieces and share them with her? No, that part was real, she realized dreamily, as Matthew talked on.

Oh, the accident? Not uncommon. The stunt man had failed to show. "The horse was broken but I wasn't—except for the leg," he grinned.

How like a little boy he looks! Bliss was surprised at the wave of tenderness that welled up inside her.

"But the other part—the complications?"

Matt waved his hand in a way that made them disappear. "Nothing the Lord and I can't handle."

Bliss chewed on the piece of steak Matt had placed on her plate. "You believe in the supernatural then—or is there a better word?"

Would he laugh at her ignorance? Thankfully, no. His voice was low and serious when he spoke. "I do believe with all my heart, if you refer to the infinite God and His Son?"

Bliss answered the question in his voice the only way she knew how. "I don't know what I mean," she said honestly. What was it Grandmother had said the day Bliss had run away? Something about there being things one could not see or explain, but that did not deny their existence. Bliss wondered for the first time if the "peculiar" old lady, undoubtedly ignored and lonely, had been searching for what Matthew had discovered. And then Matt was speaking again.

"It was God Who gave me the vision, Bliss."

"Can you tell me what it was," she begged. Matt's vision seemed terribly important.

"If this treatment works—I mean, when my leg is well—I want to do more than hang around waiting for some bit part. I want to produce my own show, a Christian film with a gentle love story combining the spiritual love of the Creator. Sound romantic and inspiring?"

Bliss almost choked. There came to her the image of the patriarchs with long beards and flowing robes preaching on some ancient-city street corner. She had seen *The Ten Commandments.* Did he mean Moses?

She realized then that she had missed part of what Matt was saying. "—just ordinary people, you know, like you and me meeting like this—"

Bliss felt her heart soar to a higher altitude. Matthew, the beautiful Matthew, and *her*? How could he hope to breathe credulous life into her ugly being and retiring personality? She was unattractive, simple—

No, she wasn't a simple person at all. For the first time, Bliss realized the complexity in the filigree of her emotions. Why, today she had felt, was feeling this minute, a myriad of emotions that she thought existed only on a movie screen. And she wasn't *stupid*-simple!

Now, for instance, she found herself nodding in agreement and understanding. Already, she was seeing the beautiful sets—daisy-dotted meadows, a church in the wildwood with fat cherubs leaning down, and cloud castles presided over by Lord and Lady Stardust...

The loudspeaker crackled and the captain's voice announced that the plane was beginning its descent. New York. Another world. How many had she been in today? The world ahead would be strange, new, and frightening. She would face it totally alone. Here, high in the clouds, there had been Matthew—Bliss wondered vaguely what his last name was, this man who had made her forget herself.

Still standing on the rim of the dream, she turned to ask him. Then quickly she clamped her mouth shut. The world she was about to enter was the real world. Hard. Cruel. Uncaring. She had to be uncaring, too. Only not now. Not when the beautiful man beside her was reaching for her hand, holding it as if to press something inside her palm. Wasn't she entitled to just a final moment in Paradise—a place she had never visited and would never see again?

And so drifting halfway back into the world where dreams come true, Bliss allowed her fingers to close around something rectangular and smooth. A book? That was it. A small book of some sort. No exchanging addresses!

"I want you to have this. I always bring a copy along. It's the *Book of Psalms,* my comfort in time of trouble. Are you familiar with the writing of David—or have you met the 'man after God's own heart'?"

"Not in person," the new Bliss said mischievously and then regretted what Matt might interpret as a flip answer.

But before she could explain, he spoke. "Forgive me, Bliss—I didn't mean to talk down to you."

Apologizing? This was a different sort of man than she had ever known. "Oh, Matt, you didn't —it was I—"

Something in the strange stratosphere in which she floated told her that Matt's eyes were on her. They were lighted as if by burning stars streaking across the firmament. For a split second all else faded away. The past. The future. Her mission—even her body, except for her eyes. They were there burning in their sockets as they locked with Matt's. There was fire within them, burning as Matt's burned, in a way she could not understand.

There was a sigh of intaken breath—hers and his—as Matt lifted the chair arm between them and reached for her. Without a word, he folded his arms gently around her. Bliss felt herself tremble as he swept the long hair from her face and cradled her as one cradles a child.

"Bliss, dear sweet Bliss, how good of God to send you my way. It has been so wonderful sharing dreams with you. If I can—if the—when my business in New York is completed—"

From the warm haven of his chest, Bliss tried to protest. "Matt—you mustn't—I—"

"Shh-h-h!" Matt laid a silencing finger on her lips. "More than anything else, Bliss, I want

you to meet *Him* in person. He's the One
who matters most of all.

"Him?"

"The Lord."

She must pull herself away, come out of this
trance. They were on dangerous ground. Bliss
knew little about "meeting the Lord," as Matt
phrased it. But if he meant religion, didn't one
have to keep a hard-and-fast set of rules to
qualify? It was like playing tennis—wasn't that
what Mother said when Grandmother took her
to church? Too many balls outside the court and
you were out—forget the "love" bit. Well, meeting a Referee was out right now. It wouldn't work
in with her plans at all. How could she confess
about Jason, what he had done to her, and what
she had in mind as sweet revenge?

"Don't look so startled," Matt laughed softly.
"I'm not going to push you into anything until
you are ready. I want you to share my vision,
Bliss. I know this has been a surprise to us both—
but I never knew there was someone out there
as sweet as you. If you feel as I do?"

He pulled her gently back to him. *Oh, yes,
Matt, yes,* her heart cried out. But her logical
mind said something quite different. *No, no, it
can never be!*

She must protest. Now! While there was time
and she had the strength.

With a little cry of despair born of a broken

heart, Bliss pushed against Matt's chest, her hands faltering when she felt the heavy beating of his heart.

"It's all a dream—a cruel joke! We—we—" she struggled to hold back the sobs that rose to her throat, then forced out the words that must be said. "We've hardly met—and you—you—*couldn't* be interested in—in me—"

Grabbing her wrists, Matt held them so tightly she felt her fingers tingle for want of blood. "*Interested!*" He spat the word out furiously, then softening, he went on, "Why not? Just tell me why not."

Bliss's head shot up. All right, she would tell him. "I'm ugly," she said.

"You're beautiful."

All courage was drained from within her. Beautiful. She was beautiful to somebody—no, to the most wonderful man in the world. Gone were the good intentions and suddenly Bliss was back in the strong arms, sobbing soundlessly. All sorts of strange emotions churned within her being. But, above it all, she was glad—oh, how glad!—she hadn't told him about winning the contest and that she was on her way for a total new look. It would have spoiled this wonderful moment that she must treasure forever. This perfect stranger had said the words, the magical words, she had waited to hear from somebody all her life.

"You're beautiful," he had declared. And, now, to herself Bliss added, "Just as you are." They would never see each other again when this flight ended. But this wonderful man had seen something within her that outer flaws could not mar. And with that she would be satisfied. Always she would know that somebody saw the inner beauty that needed no transformation.

"You've changed my life," she murmured.

"And you've changed mine." Matt had no way of understanding that they were speaking separate languages. He was wiping her tears away and fishing for something inside his pocket.

Bliss closed her eyes, trying to muster strength to let him know that nothing was left to say except "Good-bye." She could hear the scratching of a pen as he talked.

"This is all I could find to write on. It will show you where I am—say," he interrupted himself, "I've forgotten to ask how long you will be here, how I can reach you, and whether this is a business or pleasure trip."

"I don't know how long," she answered tonelessly. Purposely, skipping his question about where she would be staying, she answered truthfully, "Sort of combined business and pleasure, I guess."

Matt didn't seem to notice her change in voice. "Here is the card—"

Bliss did not open her eyes.

"No, Matt—" Was that tiny voice hers?

"Bliss, listen to me! I know that something is troubling you. But we've only a few minutes before landing and we can't waste it on things we can work out together later. We need each other. Why, you have become a part of my vision—can't you understand that I've never shared it before, that you are special to me?"

"No!" The tiny voice that was hers had gone harsh.

Matt inhaled in a way that was a near-groan. "Why, *why,* WHY must you torture yourself? Do you think I am so fickle as to concentrate on one imperfection of face or figure and not see all the others?" He hesitated before going on. "There's more you haven't told me, isn't there? Now is the time."

"No—yes—I can't talk about it!"

The seat belt warning light flashed on. There was a crackle of static. And then the captain's voice announced, "Ladies and gentlemen, we are circling the city just prior to landing at Kennedy Airport. Since this is home to me, I welcome you to New York—"

His voice drifted away in the excited "Oh's" and "Ah's" of passengers exchanging exclamations over the lighted city below. A deep sense of loss settled over Bliss, something akin to the black veil she had worn when she boarded the plane—before Matt and the short-lived exhilaration he had kindled. For awhile up there in the heavens it was as if some power had healed her, removed the ugly blemish on her face and in her heart—and let the beautiful daydream come true. But now—now, she knew it was as Matt had said, "Dreams are just that. No more. No less."

The plane hit the runway with a bump. *Quite a contrast to takeoff, which was to be expected,* Bliss thought bitterly. Dropping down from the sky is harder than soaring to the stars. Here there were no stars at all. Just artificial lights and, yes, artificial hearts, too. The bright bubble in which she had encased herself burst.

Determinedly grabbing at the veil she had crammed into her bag, Bliss drew it over her head and secured it with the pillbox hat. She was about to slip on the enormous dark glasses when Matt's hand restrained her.

"Don't," he pleaded above the shuffle of feet as over-eager passengers jostled against one another, "please don't—you have beautiful eyes."

"Nobody ever said that before," she said more to herself than to Matt.

"Nobody ever saw them shine as I did."

Shaking free of his hand, she jammed the glasses on behind the protective veil. "We must go—"

Bag in hand, Matt stepped back to let her

pass. And then they were walking down the aisle.

Outside, there was a stunning blast of humidity. Her travel suit was crushed and limp. *I'm wilted,* Bliss thought, *like a hothouse flower plucked from its stem. Lifeless.*

It took all the strength she could muster to forge ahead of Matt. There must be no good-bye . . . it was imperative . . . and somehow she was lucky. Until they reached the gate. There he caught up with her. He wheeled her around, forcing her to face him. She saw the pinched look around his nostrils again but hardened her heart.

He was breathless, too, one part of her knew. The other part knew she must escape. She dare not listen.

But the grip on her arm was like hardened steel. "We have to meet again." Without intending to, Bliss looked into the kind, sand-colored eyes that searched her face. Then, in confusion, she turned away. "Why must you run away— and turn away?" Pleadingly, he asked it.

"I turn because—" Bliss began and then stopped. It was no longer the birthmark she wished to hide. It was fear of what her eyes might reveal to this near-stranger. Only, he wasn't a stranger! It was as if she had known him forever. Dangerous thinking—

Eyes averted, Bliss went on weakly. "You

know why I turn away." The words ended in a whisper.

There was a pause broken only by the sucking in of Matthew's breath, the little mannerism she had come to recognize and, yes, to love. Just as she loved everything else about him! The thought was so frightening, a tremor ran the length of her spine.

When at length Matt spoke, it was to say, "We *will* meet again." His words, so softly spoken, were a promise.

"I doubt it—there's no reason—"

"There's *every* reason and I don't doubt it at all!"

Bliss pulled away frantically and pushed into the crowds of hurrying feet, tears streaming down her cheeks behind the dark veil. This man was too sincere, too noble, too fine to be drawn into a deception such as she planned.

And then her body would no longer obey. As if activated by the throwing of a switch in her heart, Bliss found herself turning to search the impersonal faces of the milling crowd. Surely it would do no harm to wave. But catching a glimpse of him would be unlikely.

She was about to give up when suddenly his broad, tweed shoulders seemed to loom out of the crowd. Only they were bobbing up and down foolishly, causing her to squint and try to bring her eyes in focus. It was after the blonde head disappeared altogether that the awful truth came to Bliss. Matt was far more crippled than she had realized. The thought filled her with remorse, tenderness, and regret . . . maybe she should run after him . . . maybe she was wrong . . . and they could work things out as he had said . . . maybe . . .

But no! They were of separate worlds. "Up There" had been different. The two of them had no bodies, just spirits, visions, and dreams. "Down Here" they were of the flesh, earthlings who had to survive in a harsh world. She had a commitment with *Tomorrow* magazine. And afterward, another commitment—the one to herself. Ah, revenge would be sweet. Jason Blackwell deserved what he was going to get. And with that thought the all-consuming fury of a woman scorned again wound its ugly arms around her.

And so it was that Bliss did not hear her name called frantically as she hurried toward the exit or see Matthew Thorson trying to divide the crowds in a painful effort to reach her. Someone would meet her there in one of the magazine's limousines. Just have her identification ready—

Her identification! Somehow, even before she began fishing in her bag unsuccessfully, Bliss knew that the needed papers would not be there. But they *had* to be! Otherwise, what would she do? They weren't, of course. Panic-stricken, she hesitated a moment, and then, remembering the name of the hotel where the editor had said she would be staying, she hailed a cab.

"The Hotel L'Clerc," Bliss said, trying to look and act natural.

What if there were no reservation? What if the editors had meant it in the strictest sense when they wrote that she must bring copies of the papers and letters, the contract, and a copy of the photograph she had submitted when she entered the makeover contest?

Suddenly, Bliss was aware that the driver had asked her something and that the taxi meter was eating into her small cash reserve and going nowhere. The man was looking at her strangely, too. The veil maybe? Better that than the looks she would get without it.

"Did I understand y'right? Hotel L'Clerc?"

"That's correct. Is there something wrong?"

The man only shrugged, but something in his manner suggested, "You don't know what you're in for, lady."

Oblivious to the honking and screeching of tires as the endless lines of yellow cabs fought for right-of-way, Bliss leaned back and tried to put some semblance of order to the day. It was no use. It was all too unreal.

And then they were there. At least, the driver had stopped.

But surely this could not be the right place.

Why, it was palatial! No wonder the driver had looked at her strangely. Anybody would know she didn't belong here. At the thought, fear clutched her heart.

If she didn't, she would know soon enough. And what would she do then?

Chapter Four

*H*ottest day on record—night's not much better," someone was saying. Bellboys were moving here and there. Sleekly-dressed guests moved past like manikins, no visible expression on their faces. But Bliss stood dumbfounded in the doorway. What on earth was she doing here? She was blocking the door. She must move.

"Brownout all over the city—may I help you, miss—er, ma'am?" *Ma'am?* Stunned, she did not look up.

On wooden legs, Bliss moved through the maze of faces, feeling her feet drag in the deep pile of the carpet. A dark-suited man looked up when she approached the desk. Visibly surprised, he asked politely, "Have you a reservation?"

"Yes," Bliss managed boldly. "I am Bliss McVay. *Tomorrow* magazine—"

The man was suddenly all smiles. "Oh, yes, yes, we have a suite reserved for you, Miss McVay," he beamed. "And if there is anything—"

Bliss murmured a thank-you and moved away, sickened. The dapper little man was no different from the rest of the male population, she thought bitterly. Bliss McVay in the rumpled suit, her face hidden by a somber veil, was someone to ignore or ridicule. But Bliss McVay from *Tomorrow* magazine carried clout. A woman to be catered to. Admittedly unattractive, maybe eccentric, but important.

Under different circumstances Bliss would have been overwhelmed with the tenth-floor suite. But it had been a marathon day and she was aware, as one is aware in a dream, of deep, cushiony chairs, heavy drapes, and a maze of lights which, even turned on low, added a feel of heat to the leaden evening. Air. She needed air. Space to breathe. Even the breath of the air conditioner seemed stale.

She unbuttoned her suit jacket, tore off the headdress, and kicked her shoes aside. Surely a shower would lift her from this state of depression. It was senseless to feel this way. Why, she should be happy. Wasn't she on her way to become the woman she had always wanted to be? No! The negative chord of response surprised her so much she stopped short of entering the elegant bathroom with the sunken tub and gold-plated faucets. What was the matter with her?

Aimlessly, she let her eyes drift around the rooms, filled she realized with bowls and vases of cut flowers. Hothouse plants with forced beauty. The thought angered her. What was wrong with that? Wasn't it all right to force a bloom when nature withheld the gift? And what was wrong with a girl's wanting what nature had denied her? All women should be beautiful—or *drowned!*

Hating herself for the tricky comparison the flowers had evoked, Bliss turned from the odorless blooms and hurried to the glassed-in shower stall. It was her face, her life—and her choice to be whatever she wanted to be.

No! Again the word came. A man should love a woman for what she was inside . . . see the inner beauty . . . *oh, why did I let Matt go—why, why, WHY?*

A new sort of hurt welled up within her. Wishing with all her heart that she shared his faith so she could pray that this Lord of his would bring him back, give them one more chance, she turned the shower on full blast.

It seemed only fitting that the air conditioning should falter, make a false start, and then stop completely as Bliss toweled herself dry. Fitting, too, that none of the windows would open to freshen the stale air. Leaves on the flowers drooped and it was easy to imagine that ice around the champagne would have melted. Well, she didn't want its false glow either. Her depression deepened.

But why did she find the heat so oppressive? Was it her mood or was it something more? Something she tried to remember and at the same time tried to forget . . .?

And then it all came rushing back. The night of the company ball for which she had dressed with such care. She would charm Jason, become a captivating person, the someone he had never met. And in the dimness of the soft light the unsightly blemish on her face would not show.

But the atmosphere of the Rose Room of the posh hotel had been no more suited for her hoped-for storybook ending than the private office in which she worked. Oh, Jason danced with her to be sure, holding her an arm's length away, his eyes searching for someone else as the vast herd of employees and invited guests gyrated senselessly under a mirrored globe which spun out artificial color as the spotlights bombarded it. Garish. Harsh and unreal. Bliss had wondered if the merrymakers weren't of the same fiber. Was anybody happy? And, yes, silly girl that she was, she had wondered if any of them were in love. In love the way she thought love ought to be.

It had been one of those humidity-filled nights that San Francisco seldom experiences, Bliss recalled. Jason had wiped his face when the dance ended, murmured something, and moved away as he spotted the person his dark eyes had been looking for.

The girl was a stranger to Bliss. Was she new at Blackwell & Son's Interiors? It was easy to see why any man would be captivated by the girl. She had the magnolia complexion that speaks of the Old South, the kind that would never tan deeply even if exposed to the sun. A wealth of blue-black hair framed the doll-like face and the blue-gray eyes seemed to catch every light the spinning globe above had to offer. But they were hard and cold until they met Jason's. Was it the light or didn't they change color as she arched her swan-like neck to gaze up at Jason?

"Who is she?" Bliss had wondered aloud.

"Lili Ann Paget," one of the other secretaries told her. "Fresh from Tenn-uh-see, shugah! Not that the name has anything to do with it—the last one, that is," the girl said sarcastically. "She plans to change it to Blackwell, no less."

"Jason?" Bliss had whispered through stiff lips.

The other girl shrugged. "Either one would do, Jason or his father. Claims to be a 'sure-enough ca-reah girl,'" she mimicked, "with eyes on the family fortune, if you ask me!"

Bliss waited on the sidelines. And waited. So long that it became embarrassing. And, then, feeling like the unattractive, unwanted person she had accepted herself to be, she had escaped the silly charade of it all. Outside, the air was heavy with orange blossoms, an odor Bliss loved. She buried her burning face in the nearest clump of waxy blooms, taking solace from their fragrance.

"You aren't going to get him, you know," she whispered to the remembered image of Lili Ann Paget, making herself believe it. Jason would see through the skin-deep beauty of this scheming girl. Didn't she, herself, have every advantage? She was in the office with him for extended working days which often spilled over into the night hours. One day he would come to see that she was as indispensable in his private life as she was in the office. She would be as devoted a wife as secretary. Only one thing troubled her . . . the dreams . . .

Lili Ann, a cousin of the head buyer for the firm, had experienced no difficulty in landing one of the better jobs—qualified or not. What she lacked in intelligence, Bliss decided, the girl made up for with conniving cleverness. Bliss, who had always been modest and humble, found herself taking satisfaction in her own superior mind. At least the ambitious newcomer would be no competition for her position—the position that she loved because it kept her close to Jason.

But Lili Ann saw to it that anything requiring Jason's signature needed to be brought in person. At first, Bliss headed her off with the usual, "I'll take care of this for Mr. Blackwell." And then the other girl learned the exact timing of Bliss's coffee breaks and rushed the all-important papers then. Bliss had been furious when she made the discovery. Dressed in a crisp white linen suit with a peplum over the shapely hips, Lili Ann—looking as contemporary as tomorrow—was lingering at Jason's desk, pretending to make sure that everything was signed. But her feigned innocence, her little breathless apology for intruding, and look of utter helplessness made it impossible for Bliss to say anything. And, besides, Jason seemed totally engrossed in the papers. . .

Oh, they had been clever! Going over the memory as she pulled on a cool light-weight robe, Bliss felt the familiar stirring of bitterness in her breast. He deserved to be paid back. And so did that woman!

That woman? Bliss stopped dead in her tracks. The voice! Of course, she should have recognized it immediately as Lili Ann's. She had heard that low, intimate laugh before. So she had won after all . . . wasn't she in Jason's arms . . . and wasn't he making cruel jokes about his secretary, whose only weapon was a good mind? Oh, the humiliation of it all!

From where she stood, Bliss saw herself reflected in what seemed to be a hundred mirrors. The ugly purplish birthmark stood out garishly against her white face. But she was no longer afraid. After all, they were doing wonderful things with makeup these days and *Tomorrow* magazine would know them all. She would have a new face, a new life—

No! For the third time, the mocking word came from some far corner of Bliss's mind. For a split second she was unable to think why . . . and then the awful truth struck home.

There was going to be no magical makeover now or ever. Her papers were lost. She had no identification. And *Tomorrow* magazine's number was unlisted, the editor had written. The letter gave the number Bliss was to call. But the letter was lost, too.

Sinking onto the circular bed, Bliss burst into hopeless tears. And then an anger such as she had never known came, causing her to beat the pink satin pillows with tightly-clenched fists.

When she was too weak to struggle any more, she sank wearily into the ruffles of the quilted spread. Life wasn't fair. It simply wasn't fair. No matter what Matt said—

Matt! Suddenly she sat upright, fatigue gone. He had helped her collect her belongings when they spilled on the floor of the plane. He would be able to help.

And, just as suddenly, she sank back into the hollow her body had made in the satin spread. There was no way of getting in touch.

Oh, why had she been so foolish as to reject *him?* When a woman finds the one man who is right for her, why isn't she geared to sacrifice all else and let love take over? Together they could have overcome her insecurities and she would have stood by until his leg crisis, whatever its nature, was met. Together they could have given substance to the beautiful vision Matt had . . . with his producing the Christian romance film and her doing the sets. A background person by nature, why that would have been wonderful.

Tears spilled anew from her eyes. Fascinated, she watched the great, hot drops splash onto the spread, her unfocused eyes imagining that they were drops of blood squeezed from her heart.

"John Greenleaf Whittier was right." The words were torn from Bliss's aching throat and heart, " 'For all sad words of tongue or pen, the saddest are these: *It might have been*'!"

The lights flickered threateningly. Maybe there would be a total blackout. That would be fitting, she thought with despair. And then she was overcome by a strange fear and forboding. It had to do with more than the possibility of darkness. It was a feeling of imprisonment, which was foolish since she would be going home tomorrow. True, her mission would be unaccomplished, but at least she would not be stranded—

And then the awful truth struck somewhere inside her emotionally-exhausted body. The plane ticket! Oh, dear heavens, the return fare was clipped to the lost papers.

Maybe . . . just maybe . . . but digging into her purse failed to produce the needed ticket. She must have all of fifty dollars in traveler's checks and the money she was saving for a down payment on a condo was in a savings account.

Almost hysterical now, Bliss clawed at the bag's contents, breaking a nail, and twice jabbing her hands against sharp objects. And then she dumped the entire contents into the center of the bed, beside her. Nothing.

Almost unaware of her motions, she picked up the mirror, comb, and assorted notes, glasses, and pens—examining each as if she had never seen it before.

And then her eyes fell upon something different. What was this? *The Book of Psalms* . . .

Oh, yes, the little book Matthew had given

her on the plane. She was about to put it back into the bag when something dropped in her lap. A card?

At first, she glanced at the meaningless name of some surgeon with no interest. Probably something Matt used as a bookmark. Bliss was about to discard it when something on the back caught her eyes. Writing. Somebody had scribbled a message. But it was of no consequence to her what the doctor may have written. For some reason, she read it anyway—feeling that she was invading some unknown person's privacy. And then she read it again, trying to let the information sink into her foggy brain. It was incredible!

"Height, 6'2"; Weight, 180; Age, 28; Marital Status, single; Religious Preference, Protestant; Vocation, bit actor—with a vision! Read Psalm 121." And it was signed *Matt.*

Incoherently, Bliss found herself thinking, *He's here . . . Matt's here . . . somewhere in New York . . . and somehow we are communicating . . .*

That made no sense. It was as crazy as the rest of this day, week, year—or however long it had been since she left San Francisco. And for the first time Bliss wondered what time it was. Her watch showed—could that be right?—2:00 A.M. Yes, given the change of time—

The lights flickered again and then again until the rhythm became steady like the fireflies she remembered at her grandmother's house. Where could that have been? There were none of the romantic little insects in California. There was so much she wondered about. But right now she must get some rest for tomorrow and whatever it held.

As her hand rested on the fluttering bedlight, Bliss had the strange notion that there was something she had left undone. And then she realized that she was holding Matt's little gift, *The Book of Psalms*, in her hand.

Curiously, she thumbed through the pages until she found Psalm 121. To her irritation, the lights began dancing crazily, so that often the words blurred together. But doggedly she read on:

> I will lift up mine eyes unto the hills, from whence cometh my help. My help cometh from the Lord, which made heaven and earth. He will not suffer thy foot to be moved: he that keepeth thee will not slumber. Behold, he that keepeth Israel will not slumber. The Lord is thy keeper: the Lord is thy shade upon thy right hand. The sun shall not smite thee by day, nor the moon by night. The Lord shall preserve thee from all evil: he shall preserve thy soul. The Lord shall preserve thy going out and thy coming in from this time forth, and even forevermore.

Then, without further warning, the light went

out. Somehow, Bliss knew without drawing back
the drapes to her outside window that the city
below lay in darkness. There would be com-
plaints, desperation, and panic. But in her heart
there was a strange sort of peace, quite inex-
plicable really—this sudden tranquility—much
like, she thought with a little smile, Grandma's
"Other Presences" which didn't have to be seen
to be believed.

No longer fearful of the dark, she allowed her
heavy eyelids to close. As sleep began to gather
her in its arms, she thought it odd that with all
mankind's know-how this vast city lay in total
darkness. It was in need of a source of power . . .

Source of power . . . Grandma and Matt were
right, weren't they? There *was* a Powerful
Force . . . maybe down here . . . maybe up there.
Bliss tried to remember if she really had asked
that Power to send Matt back. But sleep had
come . . .

Chapter Five

The shrill peal of a bell awoke Bliss from a deep sleep. It took a full minute to collect her thoughts before she was able to fumble for the telephone concealed behind a bouquet of wilted asters.

"Yes?" she murmured, realizing that her tongue was thick as if she had been drugged.

"Good morning! This is Matthew Thorson."

Oh, Matt, as if you needed to tell me . . . I'd know that wonderful voice anywhere . . .

Aloud, she said, "Oh, Matt—Matt—how did you find me?"

His laugh was as low and intimate as she remembered. "I told you we would meet again.

But you must believe me that I had no inkling the stewardess would bring me your lost papers. I was going to try reaching you through your job—what? Excuse me a second, Bliss—"

Bliss waited. Above the wild pounding of her heart she heard some sort of muffled conversation going on between Matt and another man. Snatches reached her ear.

"Yes, it *is* important—and I am hurrying— gurney on the way—all-day procedure—the leg—"

When Matt's voice came back on the phone Bliss could detect the strain. "I must hurry, darling (*darling, had he said Darling—to HER?*) as I have an appointment and—"

"Matt, don't hang up! It's your leg, isn't it?"

"I have two, They come in pairs!" (Matt, wonderful Matt, calling to reassure her when he was about to undergo some sort of crisis. This she knew intuitively.) "But, about you, Bliss—your papers are there at the desk. I sent them by special messenger as I am tied up for awhile. And now I must go—"

"You saw—you know—and it makes no difference?"

"Nothing would make any difference, dear sweet Bliss. I tried to make that clear—oh, I see I have company—"

"But I wasn't open with you," she whispered desperately, "and, Matt, *please*—who are the people with you? I need to know—"

"And I wasn't completely open with you either—"

Matt's voice trailed away and then there was a buzz at the other end of the line. Someone had jerked the phone from his unwilling hand. Who? And what did it all mean?

Helplessly, she whispered into the dead telephone, "Oh, Matt—Matt, my darling—how can I reach you—except to read Psalms? And I will—oh, I will—"

Bliss longed to curl into a fetal ball in the middle of the great bed, letting its satiny smoothness comfort her until somehow Matt was in touch again.

But life, no matter how disappointing and frustrating, must go on . . .

A quick call to the hotel desk brought the papers she needed for the day. Phoning the number listed on the editor's letter brought the promised limo. A quick ride through the waking city and Bliss stood on the doorstep of adventure in front of the plateglass-and-chrome offices of *Tomorrow* magazine.

I should feel excited. Or scared. I should feel SOMETHING.

But there was only a strange sense of unreality about it all as she was ushered from one place to another in preparation for what a sober-faced woman in white told her was the "screening."

"We need your weight, Miss McVay . . . your
height . . . here, let me snip a lock of your hair
from underneath where it won't show . . . turn
this way, please . . . walk across the end of the
room . . . and we'll need a photograph for skin
tones . . ."

Bliss moved from one station to the next, seeing nothing, hearing nothing, just responding
automatically. Then, suddenly, she was standing
before a woman she realized to be of great importance to the magazine.

"Madame Francois," one of the girls had
whispered in awed tones at the door and then
disappeared to let Bliss do her own knocking
and introducing herself.

Madame Francois acknowledged her presence with the smallest of nods. Her gaze was
steady and unreadable, but Bliss knew that she
was under a microscope. As usual, she flinched
and turned her "good side" toward the woman.

"Turn around!" The voice was sharp and carried a French accent.

In turning, Bliss found herself face-to-face with
a woman in her late seventies. Not very tall, she
gave the appearance of added height because
of her straightness and quick, nervous move-
ments. She wore a gray silk dress with prim
white collar and cuffs. High heels, of course. But
what caught and held Bliss's attention were the
numerous rings on her fluttering hand—spark-

ling, flashing, almost alive, she thought, seeming to reflect in the thin skin of the blue-veined hands. The white hair, cut modishly short, was permed to cover her head in a cap of tight curls. Almost blue in color, it blended fascinatingly with the blue veins of her hands and the blue-white flashing of the diamonds. A blue and white creature from some universe Bliss could not imagine. . .

Her thinking was cut short by Madame Francois's no-nonsense voice.

"Thank you for having better than average sense!"

Bliss was speechless. Then, to her surprise, the woman added, "At least, you have sense enough not to chatter."

Bliss said nothing. There was no need. The woman was talking to herself.

"I don't know—I just don't know. Nobody told me about the birthmark which nothing short of surgery's going to cure!"

Then, turning to Bliss, "Why *didn't* you tell us?" she demanded.

"Because," Bliss answered truthfully, "it is why I am here. It has ruined my life and I—I—I just couldn't take a chance on being ruled out. Oh, can't you see how important it is to me?"

A cluck of the tongue. A narrowing of the pale eyes. Yes, she could see. But couldn't Bliss see, too?

"Oh, *please*," Bliss whispered, feeling the salty taste of tears in her mouth.

Madame Francois eyed her shrewdly. "Who is he?"

"He?"

"Come, come! It's always a man."

The woman's white hands fluttered, but her watercolor blue eyes were steady. A faint, exotic aura of perfume wafted about the room as if fanned by the busy fingertips. Other-worldly and strange though she was, Bliss felt drawn to her in a way she was unable to understand.

As if hypnotized, Bliss felt her own eyes meet and hold those across the polished desk from her. And suddenly she had blurted out the whole story. Her ugly childhood. The lonely growing-up years. The disappointment of no-dating teenage days. The fantasies. Then Jason. And, finally, Matt.

With head bent, like a child about to be banished from the room, Bliss waited. But, when at last she dared look up, there was no change in Madame Francois's expression. The unpredictable woman showed no sympathy. But neither did she condemn. She simply sat there chewing on the tip of a slender pearl writing pen, periodically removing it from her pursed lips to tap on the mahogany desk. At length she spoke briefly.

"You will excuse me." It was a statement, not a request.

Alone, Bliss felt the boldly-colored walls close in around her. The giant mural on the ceiling was most assuredly going to cave in on her. It was hard to breathe.

It occurred to her for the first time that the air conditioning had come back on sometime during the night as had the lights and she had been too busy with her thoughts to notice. How could such a mundane life as hers turn into the material for a novel?

Novel! With the thought, her mind flew to Matt. Automatically, she reached into her handbag and pulled out the little book he had given her. Somebody a long time ago had told her that a troubled person should open the Bible at random. The words would hold the answer. Bliss doubted that. But holding the book made her feel closer to Matt.

But, again, why not? What was to be lost by letting it open wherever it might choose? No matter what the words were maybe they would take her tormented mind off the problem at hand . . . Matt's, about which she knew little and could do nothing . . . and the deep, deep wound Jason had inflicted yesterday.

The book opened. The pages fluttered and stood still. The first verse that caught her eye read: "The Lord is nigh unto them that are of a broken heart; and saveth such as be of contrite spirit." Psalm 35:18.

Bliss closed the book and then her eyes. Could it be true? Was there a Someone who cared how much she had suffered? What she was suffering now?

"The Lord is nigh unto them that are of a broken heart . . ." Bliss repeated the verse over and over in its entirety. She was unaware when Madame Francois reentered the room.

The woman cleared her throat, causing Bliss to jump self-consciously. She had drifted into a Somewhere that had nothing to do with the here and now. What must this sophisticated woman think of her?

"Interesting" was the woman's one-word comment, as she glanced at the open book. "And now let's get back to the business at hand. We," she nodded to a closed door behind her, giving no clue as to who else made up the first-person-plural pronoun, "feel that there is only one answer. Surgery. There is a marvelous plastic surgeon here. Eccentric. Expensive. But the best money can buy—"

"Money?" Bliss's hands flew to her face in reflex action. "I—I just thought it was all free— I—"

Madame Francois shrugged. "It is the best we can offer. The other services you are right about. Free."

Bliss felt weak tears of disappointment slide through her shaking fingers. "Forgive me—it's almost more than I can bear—added to all else—"

There was a deep sigh across the desk. "You know, it's a once-in-a-lifetime opportunity. Don't let it slip through your fingers! And lose *him* as well."

"But the money—how much—?"

"A lot. Still—" There was a significant pause and then a confidential whisper, "I will talk with Dr. Teegarten. Through us, he might make a substantial discount."

Hope stirred within Bliss's breast. "Oh, would you? And I do have some—not a lot—"

The condo money, she was thinking, *wouldn't it be better spent like this?*

Madame reached for the white French telephone, dialed with the end of her pen, and spoke rapidly in French to another party. When she replaced the instrument, she turned to Bliss.

"Eight o'clock tomorrow morning. The limo will take you to Dr. Teegarten's office."

It all happened so quickly that Bliss felt sure she was not absorbing the meaning. Surgery? She was to have surgery tomorrow? And with this doctor as yet unknown to her. . .or was he? The name seemed vaguely familiar. She dismissed the idea and wondered if she should thank Madame Francois or try to pin down a fee. The scenes were changing too fast for her to keep up on the plot.

But before she was able to find a voice, the other woman was speaking.

"I'm not a Bible reader like you, but I like the words of Emerson: 'What lies behind you and what lies before you are tiny matters compared to what lies *within* you.' "

And with that she waved Bliss away.

Chapter Six

The air was heavy with an impending storm, humid air fanning her legs, as Bliss stepped from the magazine's sleek, black automobile back at Hotel L'Clerc. High above the roar of the traffic, she imagined the rumble of thunder. Even so, she felt the need to walk. To think. To try putting some meaning to all that had happened to her today.

But it was not about her day as much as Matt's that her thoughts turned to as Bliss hurried along Fifth Avenue.

Where was he now? And what had happened to him? Would he get in touch as he had promised? What did she know of him, after all, other than what he had chosen to tell her on the plane and to write on back of the card?

The card! Of course. Blessed with her photographic memory, she should have recognized the name on the engraved business card immediately. Turning on her heel, she hurried back toward the hotel, almost running in haste, in spite of the trickle of perspiration she felt running the length of her body.

If people looked at her curiously, Bliss was unaware. Something inside her had changed, she knew; but this was no time for self-analysis. Single-mindedly, all she could concentrate on was the card which would lead her, without doubt, to Matthew Thorson who suddenly had become the most important person in her life.

Back inside her room, she rummaged quickly through some of the things she had removed from her purse and placed in the drawer of the writing desk.

The card! Yes, the name was Dr. Teegarten, just as she had known it would be. The plastic surgeon to whom Madame Francois was sending her for consultation tomorrow morning. She and Matt would be reunited!

A thrill of excitement welled up inside her followed by a chill of apprehension such as she had never known before. It was as if a hill of ants had been released inside her. Maybe something more serious than she knew was wrong with Matt . . . maybe he was finished with the diagnostician. No, Dr. Teegarten was a surgeon who, she thought disjointedly, was about to dissect her face . . . maybe Matt was gone!

Almost in a frenzy, Bliss's trembling fingers dialed the number on the card. The receptionist was polite but firm. She was unable to give out information.

Hoping the telephone would ring, Bliss showered with the glass door open, then ordered a light meal sent up to her room. *Ring, ring!* Her confused mind willed the telephone; but the instrument was stubbornly silent. At last, she sent back the picked-over dinner and lay down across the bed exhausted.

Her sleep was dreamless and unrefreshing. When the alarm clock rang at 6:30 she rose, white and drawn, to find that the rain was coming down in torrents.

Wishing she were in better spirits and more excited about the day ahead, Bliss forced herself to dress in the same clothes she had worn on the plane. She had brought along only one change of clothes and it occurred to her suddenly to wonder how long this procedure, whatever it involved, was going to take. Other thoughts followed that one rapidly.

She must get in touch with her landlady. And with the office. They would be wondering where she was. Not that she intended telling them, of

course; but she would need a leave of absence
. . .no, that wouldn't work. There was no re-
course but to resign her position. That way she
could return in her new image, reapply, and—
unrecognized—charm the man who had broken
her heart in a million pieces.

Only one thing troubled her. Why was revenge less important now than finding Matt?

Today seemed but a continuation of yesterday, Bliss thought as she entered the offices of
Dr. Cedric Teegarten and Associates. Same
posh setting as yesterday in which one felt rather
than saw a large, well-trained staff who moved
with studied quiet. Strangely out of keeping were
the softly-haunting strains of Glenn Miller's or-
chestra. Tuned in to soothe the patient, she supposed, but it did nothing to lessen her agitation.
She must find Matt—

"Please," she said quickly to the first person
she saw in white, "I need some information—"

"The doctor will be with you shortly," the
woman said in a kindly tone of dismissal.

Then suddenly Bliss was surrounded by people who did a repeat performance of the pre-
ceding day. Height, weight, general health,
family history. . .wearily, she answered their
questions, donned a hospital gown, and waited
as several male voices behind a curtain talked
of centimeters, skin grafts, and White's footnotes
vs. Kingston's methods.

All this because of a birthmark?

I'd walk out, she thought wildly, *if this stupid gown weren't paper!*

But the thought died quickly for she was being ushered into the office of Dr. Teegarten— with as much aplomb as if she were about to approach the throne of "The Great Oz"!

The plastic surgeon, a short, stout man with thinning hair and a thickening middle, looked at Bliss through thick-lensed glasses. There was something akin to compassion in the neutral-shade eyes. A compassion which his brusque manner failed to reveal.

"Hmmm, hmmmm," the man kept saying to himself, and finally introduced himself and asked her to be seated beneath a cluster of blinding lights. "Hmmm, hmmm . . ."

At last he snapped off the lights. Bliss blinked in the comparative darkness and, watching little circles of their remembered brilliance dance before her eyes, she waited.

Until now, she had felt nothing. But suddenly the room seemed to whirl and she realized that a great deal was at stake in the doctor's diagnosis.

"It's operable. But it's not what I would call simple. Not *simple.*" Repetition of his key word was characteristic of Dr. Teegarten's speech pattern, she realized right away. But what did he mean by "not simple"?

"Serious, Doctor—long recovery—or, uh, expensive?"

"Yes," he answered vaguely. "*Yes.*"

Madame had said he was strange. She was right, for his words were no answer at all.

"Had another patient in yesterday from San Francisco. Better get at the operation tomorrow. *Tomorrow, yes.*"

His or hers? For there could be no doubt that the San Francisco patient was Matt. "You mean—"

Dr. Teegarten cut into her sentence. "Nine sharp."

He was about to waddle away, but Bliss put out a restraining hand to latch onto the starched cuff and hold it. The doctor looked surprised, but she had his attention.

"Please," she said desperately, "I have to know your fee. I may be unable to afford this, after all." Bliss gulped and then hurried on, "You see, I didn't plan on having surgery—just a beauty makeover—and I—I—well, really, I don't know how I got into this!"

Without warning the tears came then. Embarrassed, she let go of his hand and fumbled for a tissue in the translucent box beside the chair. "I'm sorry," she whispered.

"You have beautiful eyes. *Beautiful,*" the strange man said. "Unfortunate that they show sadness. *Sadness, yes.* But who knows but what we can change that? That is why I have never married. *Married,* you understand?"

Mutely, Bliss shook her head. What did eyes and his marital status have to do with his fee? But when he spoke, she understood.

"My love in life is to make women beautiful— *beautiful* and *happy.* Nine o'clock tomorrow. Fee? We shall *see.*"

"Doctor, the other patient—is he—"

But the doctor was gone.

Chapter Seven

T he rain had stopped, but skies were leaden as the uniformed driver turned the limo toward the hotel. In Central Park lights glistened wetly on the few remaining leaves.

Such a short time ago, Bliss thought, those trees would have stood proudly in their garbs of gold and crimson. But their glory was cut short. Like her hope of finding Matthew Thorson.

Why then didn't she feel rejected? Such a short time ago, she would have been wallowing in a mixture of bitterness, depression, and self-pity.

Now, strangely, hope clung to her heart like

the few remaining leaves. There was some explanation. Matt, handsome and appealing as he was, simply was not a male egotist who indulged in silly, meaningless single-flight romances.

Bliss trusted him. *Trust!* She tasted the word and found it sweet. She had never allowed herself to believe in members of the human race before. And here she was trusting her face, figure, and self-image to two strangers—and her heart to a man she had known all of three days. It made no sense.

Yes, it did. It made all the sense in the world, which had turned suddenly beautiful in a way that had nothing to do with rain. Why? Because "I'm in love, I'm in love, I'm in love!" her heart sang out the answer.

In that frame of mind, Bliss took out the book Matt had left with her. *Maybe I'm using it as a ploy*, she thought as she stretched out on a loveseat beside the window. *Or a way to reach out to Matt.*

And then, irrationally, *If so, Maybe that's the way it's supposed to be . . .*

First, Bliss reread a portion of the passage to which Matt had referred her. Midway she stopped; and wiggling her toes deliciously, she closed her eyes and repeated the remainder by heart. When she reached the ending, a strange warmth crept over her being which caused her to repeat the words, "The Lord shall preserve thy going out and thy coming in from this time forth, and even forevermore."

Without realizing she was going to speak, Bliss heard her own voice, "Lord, who made heaven and earth, are You really up there—never slumbering? Then watch over Matt for me. . . ."

For a single moment, behind closed lids, Bliss felt that she was not alone. This was incredible! Could this be the "Other Presence" Grandmother had spoken about? Why, it was not frightening at all. It was peaceful. . .

Bliss was so buried in her new experience that it took several seconds for her to be aware that someone was knocking on her door. Moving quickly across the floor, she realized that the tense muscles along the back of her neck had relaxed completely.

But she was not prepared for the person who stood there. It was a dream. The good one. The one with the happy ending. And she could only stand as one stands in a dream. Unbelieving. Then, believing, unable to react.

"Well, aren't you going to invite me in?"

The low, rich voice. The beautiful face. The familiar thrill of sheer joy up and down her spine. And still Bliss was unable to move.

"Oh, Matt—Matt, darling—*Matt!*"

She was laughing and crying at the same time. Surely "The Lord which made heaven and earth" had heard. . .and then, without seeming to move at all, she was in his arms, her head against the scratchy tweed jacket—his heart beating a wild tatoo in answer to the rhythm of her own.

Clinging to him as she had never dreamed she would cling to any man, Bliss realized suddenly that she had dislodged something and it had fallen to the floor. Glasses? Dark glasses? At night? Not hers. His—

"Why?" Bliss heard herself ask foolishly. As if it mattered. As if *anything* mattered.

Matt brushed her hair gently with his lips. "Why my disguise, my dear one?" he teased softly. "Don't you know that celebrities spend the first half of their careers trying to get themselves recognized and the second trying to hide their identity?"

A laugh rippled from Bliss's lips as Matt picked up the glasses, slipped them into his vest pocket, and led her to the loveseat where he pulled her down beside him.

"I wore the glasses so I could slip out of captivity—but here, I have something for you, if we haven't crushed them between us!"

Matt handed her a bouquet of white violets. Bliss took them with trembling hands and began crying anew.

"There, there," he murmured, "what have I done?"

"Something wonderful," Bliss said between

little hiccups, "You've brought me the first flowers I ever received—and they've come from the most wonderful man in the world. Oh, *Matt!*"

She buried her face in their sweet fragrance, glad that the little white flowers seemed to have held their breath until they reached her hands. Now they perfumed the room. Just as Matt's presence lighted it.

And then she was aware that Matt had taken her face between his hands and lifted it so that he could look into her eyes.

"They're shining!" he whispered tenderly. "So I know you've had a good day. Tell me all about it."

No, they're shining because you're here!

Aloud, she said, "Well, it was a strange one—"

And, in the charmed circle of his arms, Bliss told him of the events of the two days they had been apart. Actually, they had been grueling and frustrating—leaving a lot that was still to be answered. But as she talked, all that had happened suddenly became funny. Matt found every word she said amusing. They laughed at each incident and, it seemed, for the sheer joy of being alive—with Matt leaning down frequently to kiss the tip of her nose in order not to break into her report.

Why, she thought suddenly, *he finds me entertaining.* Well, maybe she was, consider-

ing the glow he had kindled around her heart.
Looking up to express gratitude with a glance,
she felt his lips claim hers in the first tender kiss
they had exchanged.

"Bliss—oh, Bliss, my darling!" There was
something akin to pain in his voice. She felt the
same stirrings. Breathing was hard. She felt—
well, just on the edge of pain herself. And yet
filled with a joy so intense and pure she wished
it were a tangible thing—a bright feather, sea-
shell, or piece of driftwood she could hold onto
forever in memory of this moment.

Never again would she experience this beautiful, soft fade-out into love's newly-discovered
ecstasy—the kind that lighted the world.

But through the brilliance of it all, Bliss sensed
something was changing right before her eyes.
Matt's arms had dropped to his sides, causing
her to sit straighter on her side of the loveseat.
And what on earth was he saying? His words
made no sense.

"—but I had to come to say 'Good-bye,' my
darling—"

"Good-bye?" she whispered stupidly, realizing that she sounded like Dr. Teegarten.

"It isn't going to work—I can't go through with
it. The risk is too great—"

Matt's eyes had changed from pewter to char-
coal again. But the way his steady gaze burned
into her own, Bliss knew that the words did not

refer to their relationship. But, of course—the leg—

"Forgive me—I didn't give you a chance to share your day. What did the doctor say—is that the problem?"

And before Matt could answer, Bliss asked another question, speaking slowly as she remembered his words. "Is that what you meant by saying that you had not been completely honest with me? You can tell me—"

But Matt shook his head slowly. And his voice was sad.

"No, I can't put you through this. It's something I must work out myself."

Abruptly, he rose. "I'm going," he said, "while I still have the courage and my self-respect."

"Please," she whispered, "*please* tell me. It's the leg, isn't it?" In desperation, Bliss realized that she had grabbed at the lapels of his sports jacket and was hanging on as one clings to life raft. "Then I'll go with you!"

"No!" The sharpness of his voice surprised her. Then in a softer tone he said, "I want you to go ahead with your plans. It's what you've dreamed of—and I want you to be happy."

"That's impossible—away from you." It occurred to Bliss for the first time that, with all their closeness, Matt had not declared his love. It hadn't mattered at the time. He included her in his plans and that had been enough.

In fact, it was she—and for reasons of vanity—who held back. But it was more than important now. It meant whether she cared to go on living. She gripped the lapels even more fiercely.

"Matt, explain to me," she sobbed, realizing that she had no pride left where her love for him was concerned, "don't you care?"

"God alone knows how much!" The words were torn from his throat like her hands were torn from his lapels. "That's why I'm saying good-bye."

And then she was alone. With the scent of violets. And *The Book of Psalms*. . . .

Chapter Eight

*B*liss turned out the lights, opened the drapes, and sat beside the window that that offered a view of the rain-washed city below. But she saw no beauty in it. And no beauty left in her life. It was as if the lights inside her, like those in the table lamps, had been extinguished. She had to sort out her feelings and concentrate hard on all that had happened. But how does one do that when nothing makes sense?

"I came here for a beautiful face," she whispered tonelessly into the darkness, "and instead I lost the little beauty I had—the little bit that only I knew existed until Matt came."

What was that old chant she used to play with other children? . . . oh, yes, "Finder's keepers, loser's weepers."

Well, she wasn't going to weep! No, she would be a finder instead. Dully, Bliss was remembering an instructor, whose name she had forgotten, demonstrating in one of her interior decorating classes. The woman had a little metal frame she kept shoving around over photographs, calling it her "finder." The implement framed squares here and there until, satisfied, the instructor would exclaim, "Ah, and here is a corner of interest! Discard all the rest and from this we shall build beauty!"

Closing her eyes, Bliss mentally moved the imaginary frame over her life. But, try as she would, there was nothing but ugliness. Then, experimentally, she tried the little game with her days here in New York. And, of course, there was Matt—wonderful Matt—his perfect face in the very center, but so tortured just moments ago.

Oh, why hadn't she forced him to let her go with him . . . made him share his secret?

Slowly, as if she were awakening from a deep sleep, Bliss realized anew that she, too, harbored a secret. One she had not shared with Matt. He had found out on his own about the new image which now seemed meaningless; but she had neglected to tell him the most important thing

of all. That it was motivated by hate, not love.
A loving relationship could never survive when
it was built on dishonesty . . . and yet she had
lacked the courage to admit the hatred and vin-
dictiveness that burned inside her.

It would have meant losing Matt. He was too
fine to love a girl who violated the rules of his
faith. And she was sure that his God would mark
it down against her, too.

A deep sadness washed against her insides—
an unexplainable emotion, except that it was the
deepest one she had ever known. For a moment, she was tempted to confess to somebody
. . . Matt was not here . . . but Somebody would
hear. Wasn't that the promise she had read in
Psalms?

"No, not yet," Bliss whispered brokenly to the
Other Presence she felt inside her heart. "Maybe
when this is over . . . he *did* tell me to go ahead
with my plans, You know," she added defensively.

Then, before she could change her mind, Bliss
switched the lights back on and looked at her
watch. Too late to reach San Francisco. She
would call the first thing tomorrow morning.
There was time even then to change her mind,
depending on how the conversations went . . .

•   •   •

The first call went routinely. She had dialed

directly to her landlady, not daring use an operator who might give her whereabouts away. Everything was fine, Mrs. Bronson said, but shouldn't Bliss check in at her office? There had been a number of calls.

With shaking fingers, Bliss dialed Blackwell & Son's asking for Jason's extension.

"Oh, please, please answer this one yourself," she whispered across the miles.

He didn't, of course. Instead of Jason's voice, there were the honeyed tones Bliss remembered so well.

"Good morning," Lili Ann Paget's greeting managed to omit the *r's*, "who's speaking, please?"

What was she doing in Jason's office? Here Bliss had been away three days and that scheming girl had managed to slither into the spot that Bliss had worked hard for three years to get. Plus having a good mind. And a knowledge of the business! A new tide of anger swept her being.

"Hello—hello, who's there?" Lili Ann said charmingly.

"Bliss McVay, Mr. Blackwell's secretary," Bliss said formally. "I should like to speak with him, please."

There was a quick intake of breath. And the charm was gone.

"Bliss McVay! Where *are* you? We've—"

Bliss cut into her words. "Where I am is unimportant. But I do need to speak with Mr. Blackwell."

"He can't be disturbed. I take his personal messages—but we will be needing to know when you will be back—"

Angrily, Bliss said, "That's my message. I won't be back. Just say I am scheduled for surgery and recovery time is uncertain."

"Oh, but wait—*wait*—you can't hang up! You see, there's been a real problem here and Jason —Mr. Blackwell—will be needing to know how to get hold of you—for questioning—"

With deliberate calm, Bliss hung up the telephone.

Bliss was fifteen minutes early for her appointment which seemed to please the receptionist. "The doctor will be with you—"

"Shortly," Bliss finished, accepting the hospital gown and turning to the room she had occupied the day before.

Almost moments later Dr. Teegarten swung open the door and entered. Bliss was tempted to ask him if he ever knocked; but she had two other questions, each of greater importance.

"Doctor, I know it violates your rules to give information about other patients. But it's important to me—"

"I don't know where he is," the doctor said bluntly.

Bliss thought in some small corner of her mind

that the wrong person might be asking questions.

"I don't either," she said softly. "We *do* mean Matt—Matthew Thorson?" When he nodded, she went ahead, "I know something is terribly wrong."

"Terribly wrong," Dr. Teegarten echoed. "And now shall we get on with what concerns you? Concerns *you?*"

It was no use. This man wasn't about to bend a rule. But the other question wouldn't violate his sacred code.

It concerns me, she thought—*correction, it concerns my case. But Matthew Thorson concerns my heart.*

"Dr. Teegarten," Bliss said slowly, "I *have* to know how much this is going to cost. I may be unable to go through with it."

The man, who claimed his only love was making women beautiful and happy, threw up his short-fingered hands in despair.

"Why is it that all my patients seem to be saying the same thing? Why?"

Matthew, she knew he meant, but the doctor was speaking, "We shall see how successful I am. See?"

No, she didn't, but she must listen to his next words. When they came, they did not concern either of her problems.

"It is time *I* did some questioning. What kind of relationship did you have with your father?

Natural father?"

Taken aback, Bliss gasped, "My father—why, I never saw him! He left my mother—I think that's how it was—and—" She paused and then said quickly, "Why do you ask?"

"Hm-m-m," he said, giving no indication of having heard her question. "And your mother? What was her attitude toward the separation? Attitude, mind you. Pride, jealousy, insecurity, hurt feelings?"

Bliss tried to remember. Mother was so much closer to Miriam. Maybe they had talked, but not Mother and Bliss. None of the words Dr. Teegarten used seemed to apply. Neither did her mother seem sad.

But there was something—what was the proper word, more like—

"Powerful," Bliss said aloud. "The divorce seemed to make my mother feel that she could wield power—only that doesn't make any sense."

"It makes sense. When there's anger there's the desire to hurt. Very powerful weapon. It takes a lot of strength to hold a grudge and sometimes the weaker ones can play the game longer than the stronger. Powerful." The doctor, busy with her files, adjusted his half-glasses. "Any grudges? You, I mean—anger, hate, revenge?"

Bliss sat down suddenly without invitation. In

another second her legs would have crumpled beneath her.

"Really," she began weakly, "I don't have to answer these questions—"

The doctor looked at her for the first time. And to her surprise there was the same expression she had read before. Compassion. And his voice, when he spoke, was gentle. "No—no, you don't. But it helps me. Most women want me to make them lovely to look at but not lovely to love. Somehow I don't want that happening to you."

The doctor's words drew Bliss to him as his manner had failed to do. In the intimate moment, she dared whisper, "Were you ever in love?"

"Once, a long time ago. A long time."

The moment was gone. The doctor closed the file and rang for the nurse.

"I can remove the mark on your face, my child, but I cannot go beneath the surface. That's where beauty lies."

• • •

The operation was over. The bandages were ready to come off. It had gone well, the nurse told Bliss. And, no, there had been no messages. Except for constant calls from Madame Francois who was eager to go ahead with what she felt was the most important part of the makeover, her own personal touch. Madame said her room was still reserved.

Bliss felt both elated and defeated. Surely the operation would be successful. Somehow she thought this strange surgeon made very few mistakes.

But she felt defeated because of being unable to hear from Matt. She had thought he would contact her. Maybe she should have prayed . . . did God hear prayers from unworthy people like her when they were about the worthy ones?

Buried in her thoughts, Bliss was scarcely aware that the nurse was snipping off the bandages while Dr. Teegarten concentrated on Bliss's right eye.

"Close," he muttered. Then, when she would have preferred a mirror, he had her following the pin-dot of light he held before her.

"You mean—you mean—my vision was at stake?" Bliss asked at last when the light was turned off.

"Could have been," Dr. Teegarten's voice was husky with emotion. "But we saved it. We saved it."

Cold fear gripped her heart. She owed so much to this man.

" '*We*,' " she said humbly. "It was you who performed the miracle."

"Not alone. Doctors never perform miracles alone. Patients help—would that all were as courageous as you—and the Almighty guides these hands."

Then, unexpectedly, Bliss was weeping. The doctor clumsily tried to wipe away her tears while speaking soothingly.

"Don't cry—it's all over now. And tears destroy my defenses. Anyway," he inhaled deeply, "here you are crying *before* assessing the damages!"

His unexpected attempt at wit touched Bliss deeply. Here was a kind man, she knew, even before he said, "Beautiful, *beautiful!*" and handed her the mirror.

Bliss hesitated, eyes squeezed shut. And then she looked at the beginnings of her new image. Breathless with excitement, she cried out, "OH—oh—oh!" Then, throwing the mirror aside, she cried, "Oh, Dr. Teegarten, I love you!"

In her new-found pleasure, Bliss did not see the look of wonder cross the fatherly man's face. Later she would recall. . . .

Chapter Nine

Madame Francois looked carefully at Bliss. "We must," she said slowly as she ran fluttering fingers though the short crop of silver curls, "decide on lifestyle and, of course, individual preferences. You know, light and airy, sophistication, or *a la natural*. Then, our experts get to work on you—under my expertise. I choose to supervise this one myself."

"Is it possible," Bliss ventured, "to make me over completely—so completely that nobody would recognize the new me—and still keep me—well, as you say, *a la natural?*"

The older woman tapped her front teeth with the end of the pearl pencil in her hand.

"We shall see. Your hair is terrible—color, length, style—*terrible!* Skin, no better. The figure will do with some shaping up—*and* some straightening up! Now, your eyes are your best feature. We'll emphasize them to bring out the yellow-topaz look—try to pick up some high-lights that should be there. Fortunately, they're wide-spaced."

Madame Francois leaned forward to sweep Bliss's hair from her face. Bliss felt herself turn away instinctively and then she turned back. There was nothing more to hide. Madame Francois nodded approval.

"Better—now face me—aha! As I suspected that hidden face is heart-shaped, another plus. Yes, we can do it." Her own face was suddenly animated. "We can!"

In the days that followed, Bliss lost all track of time. She had thought this would be easy. Instead, it required hours in the gym and "rest time" was spent in consultation with makeup artists who began a skin-care program of packs, scrubs, and massages. Then, there were the hot oil treatments for her hair . . . the working out of a nutritious diet . . . walking with books on her head. Days became twelve-hour shifts.

Bliss went back to the hotel exhausted each evening. At first, she was sure there would be a message from Matt. Something. *Anything.* Just a little crumb to put them back in touch.

The rest they would work out together. *Together.* Oh, wonderful word! Together—and in love—

But with each day's disappointment, Bliss's heart grew heavier. Was there a possibility that they would never meet again? Was Matt's love no stronger than that?

And then, when she was almost overcome by remorse, Bliss would reassess the situation. The problem lay with Matt's leg and his inability to cope with the findings of Dr. Teegarten and his consulting physicians. She must keep believing.

On one such evening, Bliss picked up her little book of Psalms and read for what seemed hours. How beautiful the words were—and how appropriate. Bliss found herself underlining and committing to memory verse after verse.

"Why, these might have been written for Matthew and me!"

Then, smiling as she showered, she mused, "Some sing in the shower. Why shouldn't I quote David's writings?"

How long wilt thou forget me, O Lord? Forever? How long wilt thou hide thy face from me? How long shall I take counsel in my soul, having sorrow in my heart daily? How long shall mine enemy be exalted over me? Consider and hear me, O Lord my God; lighten mine eyes, lest I sleep the sleep of death . . . .

Then, turning off the shower, Bliss stepped from the stall and knelt beside the pink velvet-covered stool. "Oh, Lord, wherever You are and *Whoever* You are, don't hide from me. You see, I've come to ask nothing for myself. I'm not worthy. But Matthew is one of Your servants and I ask You to look after him. Even if You and I never meet in person . . . or he and I never meet again . . ."

That night Bliss cried herself to sleep with *The Book of Psalms* pressed to her heart. The next morning she was still clutching the book. And she saw that for the first time since arriving in New York City the sun was shining. Somehow it seemed like a good omen.

"Well, I must say you are looking more cheerful!" Madame Francois said in greeting. "Are you aware that soon now you will be ready to greet this man of your fantasies in your new image? Tell me, have you decided which of them it's going to be?"

The question was startling. Which pull was stronger, her hate for Jason and the pain he had caused or her love for Matthew and concern with the pain he was suffering?

The object of her beauty makeover seemed to have changed . . . no, it hadn't changed, Bliss told herself. It was only that the hard days and her worrying over Matt had given her no time to concentrate. Well, wasn't that it?

And besides, there was no choice. Both men were out of her life. A part of the many worlds she had experienced lately.

"Well?" Madame Francois prompted.

Bliss turned away from the all-seeing eyes of the older-woman. "As you say," she murmured, "it was a fantasy."

"Nonsense!" And before Bliss realized what was happening, she was propelled to a four-way, full-length mirror. There she surveyed herself as one looks at a stranger.

What Madame Francois said was true. The course was nearly completed. Her hair was in need of cutting and styling, but it glowed with vitality. Her skin, yet to be made up, had lost its muddiness and bloomed delicately fresh and dewy. And, admittedly—tall, straight, and somewhat regal—she moved with a new loose-boned grace.

A rush of gratitude swept over her. These had become her friends, the closest friends she had ever known—Madame Francois, Dr. Teegarten, their assistants. And Matthew.

Oh, Matt, where are you? Bliss's heart cried out. *I want so much to share my new self with you!*

"I can't thank you enough—"

Madame Francois did not seem to have heard. She allowed a delicate frown to crease her forehead, then massaged the area as if to erase it.

"There is still something lacking," she said, shaking her head from side to side. "I am disappointed with the eyes. They were to have been the focal point."

"Perhaps the makeup will help."

"Makeup can only enhance what is already there." There was a touch of near-sadness in the woman's voice. "Eyes are windows to the soul!"

For the first time, Bliss wondered what the woman's private life was like. Was she lonely or—

"You are scheduled all day with our makeup artists." All business again. "After which I personally will supervise some changes in wardrobe. It's a part of the package."

New clothes? That came as a surprise. Bliss had been about to say she could afford nothing else and now this nice surprise.

But it was followed by a sudden pang of realization that Dr. Teegarten had not named his fee.

"Before I go—can you give me some idea of what the cost will be for the surgery? I—"

"Cost? Who can say what Cedric will demand? A pound of flesh maybe, not that you have any to spare."

Then with a wave of her thin, jeweled hand she motioned Bliss toward a middle-aged woman in white.

But before Bliss could follow the woman, Madame Francois hurried forward to whisper a startling question.

"Tell me, my dear, when do we know a dream is just a dream?"

"Why, when we wake up, I guess?"

"Precisely! So sleep a little longer, my child."

Somehow the words seemed significant. But the busy whirl of the day made thinking impossible. Mr. Frederic, the hair stylist. . . Agnes, the manicurist. . . Thea, the makeup expert. And all talking at once. . .

"Hair's to be cut and softly layered for fullness. . . yes, about the length of the First Lady's style. . . more fullness at the neckline. . . wispy bangs. . . the cut before the curl! Perm only where it's needed in the crown. . . *then* the highlights, taffy, maybe—yes, taffy, with shafts of sunlight filtering through. . ." Mr. Frederic seemed to command an army.

A snip of the shears. The overwhelming scent of ammonia. The crinkle of aluminum as her hair was wrapped here and there with foil.

And through it all, Bliss heard Madame Francois's voice behind her as she directed the other assistants. There was a strange note of urgency in the voice.

"Some contouring but only to emphasize the heart-shaped face, not minimize it. Draw attention to the eyes. Here, apply just a touch of shimmering earth tone. Use light neutral on the brow bone. There, don't overdo it, Thea! Keep her natural—glamorous, mysterious, but under-stated, you understand? Bisque foundation, Moonlight Plum blush and the softest Roseglow gloss. Natural—naturally, sensational, that's it!" And Bliss was certain that she heard a little gasp of awe.

The makeover must be going well.

Then suddenly Madame Francois was all aflutter.

"No, no! The brows must keep their upward tilt. See the picture? And the lip pencil is to follow the contour of the mouth as shown here!"

Bliss wondered if they could be looking at the dreadful photograph taken before the surgery. But there was little time to think on anything. The group was "ooh-ing" and "ah-ing" and someone was announcing arrival of the models with the designer clothing Madame had or-dered.

"Your moment of triumph, my dear!" Madame announced with unmistakable pride. " 'Mirror, mirror, on the wall—' here she comes!" With that Bliss felt herself surrounded by count-less people, all smiling, all eager to see her reac-tion as she stood before the full-length, four-way mirrors.

The shock was too much. Faces seemed to swim everywhere. Those of the employees. And those of the models. But nowhere did Bliss see her own.

And, then, with a gasp, she recognized the tired-looking suit in which she had traveled from San Francisco to New York—a modern-day Cinderella whose glittering gown had been changed back to sooty tatters but whose face and hair had defied the ending of the story.

Automatically, her beautifully-manicured fingers flew to her rose-kissed mouth, traced the unreconizable—and now beautiful—features, and touched experimentally the cloud of autumn-toned hair.

How had they managed to highlight it just enough to match her eyes and swirl it about the valentine-face that was no less unfamiliar? Beautiful. Beautiful and *enviable!*

With a heart filled to overflowing, Bliss turned to the group around her in hope that her face reflected the gratitude she felt. But she was too overcome to speak.

Madame Francois blew her nose delicately, then murmured into a chiffon handkerchief that the eyes were still not right. The others began boxing sponges and brushes, aids to help Bliss maintain the look they had given her.

"Hurry along, all of you, except you girls who are modeling the 1985 collection. But be seated, you girls from "Rosenquist's Shoppe." There is something I wish to discuss with this client."

Client hardly seemed the right word, Bliss thought from some remote nook in one of the many dream worlds she had entered since— since when? It occurred to her that she did not know the day of the week or month of the year. Or even the year! Maybe a century had passed. It was all so unreal—

"And you aren't listening," Madame Francois was scolding, but her voice was gentle.

Before Bliss could apologize, she continued, "You will need a new name, of course."

"Name?" What was the woman talking about?

"Certainly! A part of the new identity. You certainly cannot go back to your job as you had—uh—" She cast a furtive glance at the immobile models, ". . . planned. Let's see, what was your mother's maiden name?"

"LaBelle." The name Mother mentioned over and over, saying that she never should have let go of it.

"Strange thing," she said as much to herself as to Madame Francois, "Mother compensated her loss by adding the name onto both Miriam's and my birth certificates."

Madame Francois was delighted. "Wonderful! Then we shall use it. And your middle name?"

"I never use it."

"All the better! New identity, remember?"

"Valisa." The word was almost a whisper.

"It has a certain charm, Valisa LaBelle. Yes,
it is charming—if you are sure it shows on none
of your records?"

"I never use it," Bliss repeated.

I never use it because of its meaning.

Bitterly, she remembered the singsong teas-
ing and jeers of other children when she revealed
that Valisa meant bright and luminous. Bright,
she was, "A teacher's pet who gets all *A*'s!" they
had taunted. More hurt than angry, Bliss had
tried to explain that *bright* had another meaning, like *shining*. But they had left her standing
all alone, weeping behind her curtain of colorless
hair, their mocking words coming back to sting
like an adder. "Bright aluminum, bright aluminum, pots and pans!"

Bliss made no further effort to protest. Neither
did she attempt to explain. Only someone who
had been hurt in such a way would understand.
And then the scorn, the betrayal, the very tear-
ing out of her heart by the man for whom she
would have died. . .*yes, Jason must pay*. . ."an
eye for an eye. . ."

One by one, the parade of models passed
before her, wearing clothes Bliss would have
hoped to see only in high-fashion magazines.
Fascinated, she watched as Madame Francois
concentrated on *"The* Look," as she now called
the effect she planned.

"This," Madame Francois explained, "is the

return to the nostalgic. Oh, not to American colonialism—overdone, that one—but to the sun-baked lands of *African* colonialism! Try to envision dusty terrain and sweeping vistas," she went on dreamily.

"The collection mixes the spirit of the rugged with the romantic—shall we say, 'safari-inspired'? Days of the first missionaries. . . ."

Madame Francois bit her lip, giving Bliss the feeling that the woman knew something of the land.

Some force inside compelled her to ask, "Were you there, Madame Francois?"

"Yes, the bitter child of over-zealous missionary-parents," she said with a trace of sadness.

Then, resuming her staid role, she began to scribble on her pad, pausing to speak now and then.

"Separates in crisp linens, a California-weight gabardine suit, nubby-silk tweeds, some buttery-soft suedes and a rich madras plaid . . . and, yes, the outdoor look of the long bias-cut Zanzibar skirt—fluid look—yes, the Melbourne skirt. . . ."

Madame Francois's pencil paused.

"Monique," she said to the model wearing the skirt, "tell Fidel I do not like this blousy look. The skirt's to have stitched-down pleats—and to double-pleat the Hepburn trousers."

"Yes, Madame."

Madame Francois dismissed the models and

then turned again to Bliss.

"These are only the basics. We will pull the
look together with some heather, order another
pair of trousers in blush, some white linen
blouses and hand-painted scarves. The rugged
elegance of the turn-of-the-century safari seems
right for you."

Bliss felt herself color under the older woman's
gaze.

"Yes," she murmured. "They're perfect—"

Perfect in line. Perfect in beauty. Perfect for
her new image. But there was more.

The unbelievably elegant wardrobe seemed
perfect for the safari—her quest for two men.
One to be destroyed as he had destroyed her.
The other to be rescued from the jungle of his
emotions, just as he had rescued her. She would
bring him home and care for him until healing
was complete.

And then, oh—blessed thought—they would
be happy!

"For *Matt's* sake, Lord," she whispered. "You
see, my search is for You, too—at least, Your
blessing. . ."

"Your wardrobe will be delivered tomorrow.
Meanwhile, why don't you change into this
bush-pant suit? It's fitted correctly."

Madame Francois tossed the pants to Bliss
and pointed to where a sand-colored, double-
breasted jacket, one of its peaked lapels

decorated with sequins, hung limply.

With shaking fingers, she dressed behind the ornamental screen.

Even before looking into the mirrors, Bliss knew that the effect would be startling. Yet she was unprepared for the reflection that looked back at her.

Was her waist, girded by a wide belt, really that slender? Her legs that long? Why, she could be a model herself!

But what held her gaze was her face . . . the great eyes, picking up lights where none seemed to exist—like freshly-mined gems waiting to be cut for sparkle . . . set in a face as soft and misty as the hues of an impressionist's palette. Beautiful. Beguiling!

Then, suddenly, there was a shadow behind her. And a pair of eyes looking into her own. Lovingly. Tenderly.

"Matt!"

With a cry of gladness, Bliss turned from the mirrors.

But there was only Madame Francois, who was searching in her alligator bag for her keys in preparation for locking up.

"Come along, my dear. You will need to rest before tomorrow. Dr. Teegarten called. You are to be at his office at nine."

"But—but—" Bliss began uncertainly and then felt the familiar unreality of another of her dreams closing in around her.

At the door she paused, looking into the mirrors once more.

But the reflection was no longer beautiful.

Chapter Ten

When Bliss arrived at the hotel, the clerk stopped her. "Special delivery letter just arrived, Miss McVay. Would you like to take it or—"

Before the man could complete the question, Bliss had snatched the envelope from his hand.

Stay calm, stay calm, she begged her heart. And, *Hold me up,* she begged her knees.

Little good that it did. She found that there was such a pounding within her that surely her ribcage would burst. And by the time she reached her suite, her legs were shaking violently.

Matt, Matt! Her heart sang as she opened the door. Then, squeezing her eyes together tightly in one delicious moment of anticipation, she fell across the bed before ripping the envelope open.

Matt, oh Matt—

And then her heart sank. Even before reading the message, Bliss knew that the letter did not come from Matthew. A familiarly exotic perfume wafted from the pale yellow pages. An aroma Bliss recognized immediately as a trademark of Madame Francois.

With a heavy heart her eyes skimmed the contents. Madame Francois did not like good-byes. There ought to be a better word in the English language . . . the French had one . . . but would the beautiful Bliss, now Ms. Valisa LaBelle, know that creating the new image for her had been the highlight of her career . . . for reasons she did not care to explain? And as Valisa LaBelle, Bliss must be very happy . . . cram enough happiness into her life for the both of them, herself and that which Madame Francois had missed!

Bliss felt tears rise to her eyes and spill onto the letter. She had grown fond of the woman and all that she represented. She had done all Bliss had hoped for—and more. But neither of them could be the fulfilled woman they wanted to be. The beautiful dream was just a nightmare, after all . . .

Wiping away the tears, Bliss forced herself to read on. The words came as a shock, although she had known that time had run out even before Madame Francois told her:

> Your suite is reserved only through tomorrow, my dear, and then you must be deciding which of the young men is the true knight. The new you will win whichever she chooses, make no mistake.
>
> However, there is one word of caution. Beauty, like knowledge or love, can be used only one of two ways—to purify or to destroy! Choose carefully.
>
> Au revoir,
> Francois

"Why does it have to be so hard? Why, Lord, *why?* I don't understand—I don't—I don't—*I don't!*"

And then the tears came. Tears of fury at a God who would let these things happen just because people were too weak to live by the rules. Then tears of remorse and fear that she had broken another of the rules—maybe one which would keep the Almighty from listening to her pleas to care for Matt.

Matt! The name brought a fresh flood of weeping. She had come here wanting a makeover to get even with a man with whom she was once infatuated and now deplored. But somehow her priorities had changed. She wanted to be beautiful for Matt. She even wanted to be beautiful for Francois and Cedric Teegarten.

Oh, there was a lot to weep about!

In the midst of it all, when all traces of her carefully-applied makeup were washed away she was sure, there was a light rap on the door. At first, she was tempted to ignore it; but when it persisted, she dabbed at her face and went to see who could be wanting her.

Bliss did not know whom she expected. But certainly it was not a florist's messenger, handing her a transparent box to reveal the breathtaking bouquet of white violets!

"Who? What?" she could only gasp.

"I don't know, miss. There's a card." The boy stood waiting.

Oh, yes, here one tipped for everything. To delay him, she pretended to overlook her wallet in the large handbag.

"Yes, the card will be signed," she answered —knowing that the violets could come only from Matt.

"But what I need to know is from what address?"

She considered offering him a larger bill than was necessary as a gratuity, then decided against it. *He might think it was a bribe.* And even if he didn't, *she* did.

Well, that's one rule I can keep, she thought defensively.

The boy stood like a tin soldier.

"We at 'Worldwide Wildflowers' do not give out addresses. Strictly confidential. One of our special services!"

"Worldwide—that means the flowers could have been ordered anywhere?"

"Yes." The word came impatiently. Bliss paid him and he hurried away without a thank-you.

Bliss opened the florist's box, letting the sweetness of the violets fill the room. The words written on the card filled her heart with sweetness, too:

Thou art fairer than the children of men; grace is poured into thy lips: therefore God hath blessed thee forever. . . .

—Psalm 45:2

(And I love you!)

God is our refuge and strength, a very present help in trouble. Therefore, will not we fear, though the mountains be carried into the midst of the sea; though the waters thereof roar and be troubled, though the mountains shake with a swelling thereof.

—Psalm 46:1-3

(And I love you!)

And now, Lord, what wait I for? My hope is in thee.

—Psalm 39:7

(And I love you—forevermore!)

The card bore Matthew Thorson's name but not Matt's signature. So he might be across the continent. Or here!

Had she or had she not seen his face? But of course not. That was a part of the fantasy.

But this? This was real! "What wait I for?" meant Matt would see a doctor surely...

Bliss fell asleep that night with the violets close beside her so she could inhale their fragrance through the dark hours. The card she held close to her heart. Unnecessary since she had commited the words to memory. But the card made her feel close to—well, yes, to both of them. Matt and the God who had heard her prayers.

Chapter Eleven

❀

Dressed in the bush-pant suit, her hair fluffed in yesterday's style, Bliss sat nervously awaiting Dr. Teegarten's arrival in his private office. She was so absorbed with her concerns as to what fee he might name that she forgot completely the total transformation she had undergone since last seeing him.

The doctor entered without knocking. Bliss had become accustomed to his strange behavior and peculiar speech pattern.

He, like Francois, had endeared himself, perhaps in part because he stayed so true to form. His reaction, however, was something totally foreign to her.

"She's done it," he said as if he were unable to believe what he saw. "Done it." He wagged his head from side to side dazedly. "Her dream of reincarnation. *Reincarnation.* She's done it."

Still staring at Bliss, the surgeon took something from his breast pocket, looked at it, and lowered his voice to a whisper.

"She—*has*—done—it. Her *dream!*"

Stunned, Bliss waited for him to explain. Instead, he walked around and around her chair. More than once he pulled out what appeared to be a photograph, stared at it, and muttered inaudible words—shaking his head all the while.

At last, Bliss could stand the suspense no longer.

"What is wrong, Doctor? she asked in a wee, small voice.

Dr. Teegarten, still obviously agitated, said, "I guess I overreacted—a little. A *little.*"

Lot would have said it better, Bliss thought. But aloud she said, "I guess we all do at times. Now, if you'll just tell me what the problem is—"

"The problem?" The doctor looked confused, as if he had been asked to diagnose a disease before examining the patient. "Oh, yes, the *problem.* Here it is—one picture being worth a thousand words—"

His voice trailed off and, to her surprise and confusion, he tossed the small photograph in her lap. It was Bliss's turn to overreact.

This—this was *incredible!*

Never had she put any strength in reincarnation any more than she bothered with horoscopes and palm reading. But now an overwhelming sense of *deja vu* swept over her that was overpowering.

What could be the meaning of this? The photograph, although yellowed with age and creased in two places, was someone so like herself that the resemblance was downright spooky! Even the clothing—

"Who *is* this?" Bliss's whisper sounded ghostlike in her ears, then echoed against the walls of the office.

"Fran, my Francie—Madame Francois to you." His words, too, were a whisper.

"But why? I don't understand."

"I don't either—why she did it, that is. It always seemed important to her to go back in time—and I was never able to convince her that it was impossible. *Impossible.* We never go back. We must live it as we go—"

His face, she noticed for the first time, looked haggard. Tired. Old. And, undoubtedly, this meant a great deal to him.

Did he feel Francois had hurt her?

Hoping to reassure him, Bliss said truthfully, "I am honored—and humbled. It is a high compliment your friend has paid me—she *is* your friend? I didn't know."

Dr. Teegarten nodded without looking up. He was squinting to read the faded words on the back of the picture.

"The years have taken their toll with this—as with all else," he sighed. "Friends? Yes, *friends*—now. Once we were more—in Africa. My father was a doctor there—"

It came to Bliss then that Madame Francois had been the one love this man had mentioned when she first met him.

"I'm sorry it didn't work out," she said softly, reaching out to touch his hand.

To her surprise, he covered her hand with his own. The palm was hot and moist and the veins on his short forearm stood out like swollen rivers.

Her heart went out to him. "I wish I could help."

"Oh, you have—you have with your presence. Your presence." His grip tightened until Bliss could feel the nails of his short, capable fingers dig into her flesh. It was a little frightening for some reason and Bliss made a subtle effort to remove her hand.

She was unsuccessful. With a sudden motion that caught her completely off guard, the doctor reached for her other hand and, applying equal pressure to it, made her a virtual prisoner.

His eyes, behind the heavy glasses, were lighted by strange lights that she had not seen there before.

Something akin to panic began to form a little orbit around her heart, the circles growing wider and wider until they encompassed her entire body.

But this was ridiculous. The doctor was a kind and gentle man. Bliss was not afraid of him. Only of his mood. The strange emotions the likeness between her and his "Francie" evoked.

Allowing her hands to be still, she said weakly, "We haven't discussed your fee."

How could she manage to appear this calm when there was an earthquake taking place inside her? Foolishly, she wondered if fear—if that's what she was feeling—ever reached 10.0 on the Richter scale.

The doctor leaned forward.

"We are about to, my dear Bliss. We are about to." He appeared to be considering one moment. The next he said quietly, "Will you marry me?"

"Marry you!" The words were a faint gasp.

"I would be good to you—very good to you— the father you never knew. And you would make an aging man happy in his last days— but, no! I can see revulsion in your eyes—"

"No, no! Not revulsion! I admire you and I respect you. You have been wonderful to me— and, yes, I have come to love you as a girl loves who is in need of a father. It is only that I feel you are seeing another girl in my place."

The silence seemed to go on forever. When at last Dr. Teegarten spoke, his voice and mannerisms were normal.

"You are right, of course, very right," he said matter-of-factly. "The girl I once knew made her choice many years ago. And she was right. *Right* in saying it never would have worked—mixed marriage, so to speak."

"Mixed marriage?"

The doctor nodded. "Christian and nonbeliever. These," he said, examining his hands, "are my most valued tools. But *I* am in the hands of the Lord."

Bliss's heart had resumed its normal pace. But her mind was busy with the little "finder." Moving it from one section of the new world she had entered here. Trying to decide which was the "center of interest." Feeling a need to discard the rest. But there was nothing she wanted to throw away. Except her past in San Francisco. The past for which this present was of necessity preparing her. It was all very confusing. . .

"You believe that, don't you? You *believe* in the power of the Lord Jesus Christ and His importance in setting up the Christian home? Don't you now?"

The doctor's question, spoken so intensely, took Bliss off guard.

"I—I don't know. I mean I have studied comparative religions—but I don't know what to believe—"

"Then get knowing! It's important to young Matthew, his decisions, your marriage—you *will* marry him, I suppose?"

"I don't even know where he is. Do you—?"

"Now, about the fee. The change was remarkable. My masterpiece—and hers. Truly inspired, whether she chooses to acknowledge it or not."

Bliss chose to ignore reference to the fee for the surgery just as Dr. Teegarten had ignored her plea for information about Matt.

This man needed to be set back on his heels! With a courage the Bliss McVay who left the West Coast never possessed, "Valisa LaBelle" said quietly, "Did it occur to you that Madame Francois may have staged this very scene? That she may have arranged to send her 'reincarnation,' as you choose to call me, to you as a reminder that inside she is still Francie?"

When he caught his breath and held it, Bliss knew that she had struck an area near his heart.

"I wouldn't dare hope—" he murmured.

"Aha!" Bliss hardly knew herself that the words were coming. "Tell me, Doctor, isn't hope what faith is based on?"

"Touche!" He turned to her with a broad grin. And his face was transformed with a new light. Then, clearing his throat self-consciously, he said, "And now the fee—"

Yes, as reluctant as Bliss was to terminate the conversation, she must go. And with so much to be asked. With hands relaxed in her lap, she waited.

"What would you say to bargaining? Bargaining, that is, on a favor you could do for me, for my *clientele*—and, yes, for our mutual friend, Madame Francois?"

Bliss felt her hands tighten. She had been prepared for almost anything but this.

"Bargain?"

"I will mark all bills paid if you will consent to allow me to make use of the 'Before' and 'After' pictures. We could use them on the cover of *Tomorrow* magazine and in a medical journal article—"

But Bliss had sprung from her chair.

"No! Oh, no! Publicity is the last thing I want! Oh, please—I thought all this was confidential— please *no*—"

She was unaware that she was crying until Dr. Teegarten slapped an oversized handkerchief over her face.

"There, there, my child. I did not know how important this was. As a matter of fact, the bill has been paid in full—an arrangement made by the magazine and myself.

"Now, with one word of admonition—" Dr. Teegarten glanced at his watch, ". . . yes, I admonish you *not* to enter into something for which you will suffer like the two we have discussed today. It will boomerang. Yes, *boomerang—*"

And with that he was gone. Gone before she could thank him. Give him the kiss of farewell she had planned.

Gone, leaving her with more questions than answers.

"Consider and hear me, O Lord my God; lighten mine eyes...."

Chapter Twelve

❀

I t was good to be home. To watch the
misty fog wrap around the shoulders of the
Bay City with a silver shawl, then shrug
it off as the bright sun broke through. To gulp
in lungfuls of the tangy sea air. Listen to the call
of the gulls and inhale the perennial sweetness
of the flower-drenched air in the warmer clime.

A part of Bliss remained in New York, however. For it was there, in a great city which is
supposed to be too busy to care, that she had
found warmth and acceptance.

Bliss longed to hold the reality of it all close
to her heart, but already it was becoming a tiny
dot while the here-and-now loomed up bigger

than life. The present was what she must deal with. Getting established. Gaining reentry into Blackwell and Son's. And finding a way to destroy Jason Blackwell's ego. Making him feel the indignity, the humiliation, and—if possible—the same heartbreak he had made her feel.

So the beauty of her flight with Matt and all the wonderful things that followed dissipated like the morning fog here in San Francisco. The memory became a dream, just as the mists changed forms to make marshmallow clouds. Beautiful to look at. But high above the earth.

It would be easy to imagine that none of the incredible things happened—except for the violets!

Their sweet aroma greeted her the moment Bliss opened the door of her apartment. She could only gasp as slowly her eyes traveled around the room.

One bouquet of the violets would have been a wonderful surprise. But a roomful! On the coffee table. On the windowsills. Beside her library table . . . *everywhere!*

When at last she was able to command her body, Bliss hurried from one bouquet to another in search of a message. There was none. Instead, a card with Matt's name printed on it lay on the nightstand and the envelope bore no label.

Such a rush of warmth and love swept over Bliss that she thought for a moment surely Matt must be hiding as were some of the half-hidden bouquets.

The next moment, she was filled with an urgency to see him. Now! Surely Mrs. Bronson would know where the white violets came from. And that would lead her to Matt! She must hurry down.

Ready to lock her door, Bliss hesitated. Mrs. Bronson knew nothing of the beauty makeover. How should this be handled? And then there was the problem of her mail under her new name...

Picking up the house phone instead, she dialed the business office. A Mrs. Winchell answered to explain that the landlady and her invalid husband had gone for an extended vacation, their first ever. She herself would be filling in and if there was anything she could do...

But, no, she did not know who sent the flowers. And no, she didn't see the delivery truck either. The housekeeper accepted them at the door.

Disappointed, Bliss thanked her, explained that a Valisa LaBelle would be here, too, and hung up.

Of one thing she was certain. Matt was not playing some silly child's game with her. He would find her, he said, and he had done so.

Her address was on the papers he had located for her. And he would continue to find her because he loved her as she loved him. And then her thoughts would go the rounds again. He gave her no clue as to where to reach him. . .and he needed her. . .but what did she have to offer? His values would never condone what she had to do. . .and, like Dr. Teegarten said, "mixed marriages" wouldn't work. They just wouldn't work at all. . .

Bliss buried her face in the white sweetness of the closest clump of violets and let her hot, salty tears splash on the fragile petals. Then, sadly, she saw that the little flowers drooped beneath the shower of tears.

Like fantasies, dreams, and yes, romantically-beautiful love affairs which were not quite right, they faded away. She plucked a wilted blossom from the center and reached for the nearest book. She would press it and keep it forever.

It came as a surprise to Bliss that she had chosen the family Bible. Nobody else had wanted it and Bliss had thought it proper that someone keep a record of the family births, marriages, and deaths.

But it was not at the family history which she looked. It was the commentary in the preface of the King James Version Bible.

"Basically," it read in part, "the Old Testament

is a book of law while the New Testament is a book of love. . . ."

A book of love. She began to read then, first from curioisty; and then she became so engrossed that she read on until her eyes were too weary to read anymore.

Nowhere, she thought vaguely, *did I see a commandment except to love one another!*

Odd, nobody had explained that. . .she would ask Matt more about it. . .after her mission was accomplished here.

Was it possible to get forgiveness *before* doing a wrong? She should ask God. But what if he said, "No!"

It would all have to wait.

• • •

Outwardly poised, Bliss McVay dropped her name at the door of Blackwell & Son's Interior Decorators and moved in with all the grace one would expect from a Ms. Valisa LaBelle, lately of New York, and now applying for a job as an administrative assistant.

Inwardly, of course, she was experiencing a massive case of the shakes.

Filled with apprehension, she wondered, *What if someone should recognize me? What if I can't pull this off? What—*

Nonsense! She must get hold of herself. She had mingled in this world of thin veneer before—its false laughter and bright banter, its dog-eat-dog push up the ladder of success. If the ugly duckling could deal with it, certainly the swan could do better.

She had every advantage now. But cutting through her new poise was a sense of apprehension. She felt sad. Suddenly and strangely sad. And very, very empty inside. With grim irony Bliss remembered that just a few weeks ago her dreams had been bright and shimmering circles with Jason inside.

Well, he had taken care of that. With one sentence, he had turned her desire for him to return her love to the desire for revenge.

Couldn't Dr. Teegarten see that there was a constructive side to revenge? The kind that makes one achieve in order to prove the offender wrong? Except for Jason she would never have undergone this transformation . . . never have met Matt . . .

Matt! His name brought a wave of new sadness. A peek at her new self would help. Bliss removed her mirror and was rewarded to see that she had done as skillful a job as the artists at *Tomorrow* magazine.

And she would have been blind not to have noticed the admiring glances of the men and envious looks of the women as she came in the door . . .

"Ms. LaBelle!" Bliss jumped and realized that

the personnel manager must have called her name several times. Murmuring a small apology, she rose from the chair as gracefully as she had been taught, smoothed an imagined wrinkle from the heather tweed suit, and walked into the private door marked, ECHO PERRIS, DIRECTOR OF PERSONNEL...

It was all so incredibly easy. That evening Bliss was unable to make herself believe, even as she ran a tubful of warm water over lilac-scented bubble bath, that a firm as well-organized as Blackwell & Son's would have no heavier security.

No mention of previous employers' names, just kinds of experience and preparation; no request for her Social Security card, something which had worried Bliss; nothing at all. Just talk. And a visual assessment.

To her surprise, Bliss found herself chatting in a witty, well-informed manner. And there was no doubt but that her appearance was—well, more than pleasing to the eye.

In and out of the tub in no time, Bliss stretched out across the bed and tried to let the reality of her good fortune soak in. She closed her eyes.

Retrace it all step-by-step. Remember the past. Then maybe this unbelievable luck would seem real.

No more hunching over a typewriter, answering, "Yes, Mr. Jones (Smith, Doe or whatever

minor male employee to whom they might
assign her)". . . .no covering typewriters, hoping against hope to get away on time only to
be summoned back for late, unrewarding
dictation.

Instead of climbing up the corporate ladder,
she was executive secretary to Mr. Blackwell,
Sr., Jason's father! How did it happen? How
could it have come about?

"You have exquisite taste, Ms. LaBelle," Echo
Perris had said. "Your tests show it as does your
mode of dress and—if you will pardon me for
being so personal—so does your behavior. Just
what the senior owner is looking for. There will
be some eventual trips overseas—"

The woman's voice had trailed away. Bliss
was unable to make sense of the words.

No interviews? No anything? Just hired on the
spot! She shook her head in disbelief. The personnel director had not seemed to notice.

Lying alone in the gathering darkness, Bliss
could only assume that her new employer
trusted the woman's judgment without question.
How ironic that such a short while ago this would
have been a happy ending to the vision she had
of getting near to Jason.

Now, it was dust in her mouth. Dry. Tasteless.

Then, shaking herself angrily, Bliss came to
grips with herself, reaffirming her compulsion to
get even with Jason. By reliving the hurt he had

dealt her, the anger spread over her as she had
hoped and it was easy to start weaving her web.
The two offices joined each other. There would
be no problem. No problem—except the one
inside her heart.

Oh, Matt, what have I done? Her heart cried
out. And, then, came the awful truth that what
she was doing would drive the wedge deeper
between the two of them. But that wasn't all. . .

"Oh, Lord," she whispered to the silence
around her, "forgive me for what I am about to
do!"

•   •   •

Bliss liked Mr. Blackwell immediately. There
was a strength about him which Jason had not
inherited. In fact, Jason seemed to have inherited little from his father except his dark, good
looks.

However, although she realized from the
beginning that Mr. Blackwell was absent-
minded, she sensed that he was a man of in-
tegrity and high intelligence. Too willing to trust
his business affairs to others. Too trusting of
some people she herself distrusted.

Well, she would protect him as much as possible for the short time she would be here. As yet,
there had been no sight of Jason, which both
relieved and disappointed her. The sooner the
encounter was made the better. . . then the set-

ting of the trap . . . then out of this place. Forever!

Maybe miracles *did* happen, she would think in a dreamy moment. Maybe Matt would have the treatment and be back with her by then. And to that end she prayed night after night—always for Matt. Asking nothing for herself. She had no right. Not yet.

It was impossible to believe that God was so all-loving that He would overlook what she was doing . . . forgive her . . . accept her. And Matt deserved the best, a Christian wife—a wife who loved and trusted the Lord. Not to please Matt, but because she had met Him "in Person." Wasn't that how Matt phrased it?

But dream she mustn't! Matt and their future, if there was one, must wait. There were times, in spite of her resolve, that Bliss wanted to try to reach him through Dr. Teegarten. But a certain reserve stopped her.

Basically, I'm an old-fashioned girl, she admitted, *and I would rather he did not think I am too bold . . . when I'm free . . .*

All these emotions assailed Bliss as she adjusted to Mr. Blackwell's routine—and waited. The day would come.

It came three weeks after her return to Blackwell & Son's. Strangely, it was Mr. Blackwell himself who arranged it even as Bliss had wondered just how to bring it about.

Engrossed in a layout her employer had laid

on her desk, she did not hear the two men enter.
Then Mr. Blackwell cleared his throat.

"Ms. LaBelle, it is time you met my son—
this should have happened sooner."

Or maybe not at all. But there was no hes-
itancy in Bliss's manner. Nothing to show her
inward misgivings and fear. And nothing that
showed over-eagerness.

Just a gentle lift of her chin, a carefully-studied
tilt of her head so that the light caught the
highlights of her hair and brought out the hidden sparkle of her eyes. Business-like, warm,
friendly. But discreetly—oh, *so* discreetly—
provocative. The first impression must set the
stage.

It worked. Even as Jason took her hand in
a polite manner and said the right things, his
eyes said more.

"Father always knew how to pick them," he
said teasingly, "but this time he has outdone
himself. Small wonder he did not wait for you
to work up through the ranks. It will be a
pleasure to work so close to you, Ms. LaBelle—
Valisa, isn't it?"

Bliss turned a radiant smile Jason's direction.
"Valisa it is to both you and your father. And
please bear in mind, Mr. Blackwell—"

"Jason!"

"*Jason,* of course." She held his gaze just the
right amount of time.

"I was about to say, Jason, that I want to be a part of the firm here and that my services are available to you as well as Mr. Blackwell."

A little light went on in his eyes. Ah, yes, she had appealed to the male ego of this vain man. Not mix business and pleasure indeed!

"Oh, there will be times—" Jason said meaningfully. "Right, Father?"

The older man nodded.

"There will be—in fact, soon—but now that must wait—" He hesitated as if wondering what he had been about to say.

There was a small exchange of words between the two men. Then Jason turned back to Bliss as he was about to go.

Leaning down across the desk, he said softly, "There is something vaguely familiar. Are you sure we haven't met?"

Bliss's heart did a sommersault, then thudded so hard against the thin fabric of her ruffled, mauve blouse that she wondered if it showed. This was what she had feared in her darkest moment. This was a part of the nightmare.

But somehow she managed to murmur softly, "Oh, come, Jason, that is too old a pitch for you!"

His eyes burned into hers. "It won't be the last, will it now? We both know."

Yes, we both know . . . but Bliss only smiled.

Bliss's eyes were bright, blazing with excitement. She was overcome with a sense of power—something all-consuming and totally foreign to her nature.

But the feeling did not serve to warn her of impending disaster. No, she felt intact, whole, strong. Why, nothing could stand in the way now.

How could Dr. Teegarten have said that such planning could boomerang. . .and Madame Francois have been foolish enough to say that beauty could be used for good or evil?

Everything good was coming—well, "good" in the sense of how she had planned—if not righteous. . .

Each day became a challenge. A promise of seeing Jason. Going ahead with her plan. And each day he made a special effort to be in his father's office.

Even Mr. Blackwell commented that he had never seen his son take such a healthy interest in the new spring layouts the firm was working on day and night.

"And I have you to thank, my dear," the older man said. "You have been an inspiration to us all—lending a certain grace—an expertise we've not had before—"

Bliss thanked him graciously. The man really was a dear and she was going to be sorry things had to end this way. But some things are pre-ordained. . .or should she rethink the matter?

Could she be wrong?

Fortunately, before she could do something foolish, Jason entered.

"Hello, beautiful!" His voice lowered just enough for the words to be out of hearing distance of his father.

His too-familiar manner was disturbing. How could she have ever thought what she felt for him was love? She found everything about him distasteful.

But with contradiction, her mind—ignoring her heart—went into action like a well-oiled machine. There was a golden flush and a sudden rush of energy as though an evil spirit sat on her shoulder urging her on: "He deserves it. Go on, Bliss!"

And so the well-rehearsed words flowed from her lips.

"Why, thank you, sir, and may I return the compliment? What may I do to brighten your day?"

Jason leaned closer.

"I am about to take care of that. There is to be a buying trip and I will be in need of an assistant—"

At that moment the outer door burst open. And there stood, of all people, Lili Ann Paget. Ignoring Bliss pointedly, she focused her attention on Jason.

"Here are some important papers I need your

help on, Jason," she purred. "You know how I am—just don't understand all these nasty figures—and you always do."

For a moment, Jason seemed to waver between two desires. Then he said, "Give me a minute with my father and I will join you. Oh, you haven't met my father's new secretary, Lili. You two get acquainted and—"

Jason's voice trailed off as he stepped into the adjoining office. And immediately Lili Ann turned to assess Bliss. There was a smile on her lips which did not reflect in her eyes. Eyes that did not miss a single detail as they traveled from Bliss's shapely legs upward.

"Well, I do declare," she said in remembered magnolia tones. "I can see that the old man chose you for beauty and not brains. Oh, not that you're dumb, honey—nobody could move in this quickly and not be sly as a fox. And we *do* understand each other, don't we?"

Anger welled up inside Bliss, but she controlled it.

"I'm not sure," she said with as much civility as she could manage.

"Oh, come, come, don't be a dumb bunny! We both know why we are here. Neither of us is going to allow gossip, criticism, or office politics to deter us. Right?"

As much as she disliked this girl, Bliss felt a sudden fear of her. Obviously, they were speaking different languages, but she was suspicious of Bliss. And that could be dangerous. Better play it safe.

"I hope we can be friends, Lili." The words, so falsely spoken, stuck in her throat and she was unable to go on.

"That's impossible," Lili Ann retorted, turning toward the door. "So get this straight. He's mine!"

Chapter Thirteen

Mr. Blackwell shifted more and more of the work on Bliss's shoulders. She loved preparing the proposals for the spring showings. And loved the glowing commendations that came from her employer. It was good to design beautiful settings. Trying to imagine the beautiful people who would live in the spacious homes. And occasionally allowing her mind to think in terms of the home where she and Matt. . .but the thought was too painful. She pushed it far, far down inside her heart.

"This is where I belong" she would tell herself when the image became too dazzling. "Here with brilliant-minded buyers, talented artists,

and—well, yes—sometimes treacherous personnel. This is where I belong until . . . then . . ."

Bliss would redouble her efforts to be exactly
what Jason was looking for, wasting not a motion, not a thought.

The mission of sweet revenge became her
energizer each morning after a restless night; her
rich dessert after seeing Jason's eyes wander
from his father's office to travel caressingly over
her body, even though his undisguised passion
made her feel unclean; and her afternoon "lift"
when the deep depression threatened to engulf
her.

How could she feel so *up* and at the same
time so *down?*

The game was wearing at her nerves and she
knew that the showdown was near when Jason
leaned over to whisper, "The old man's all but
convinced you and I make a good pair."

Bliss gave him an arched look.

"Pair, Jason?"

Jason glanced over his shoulder. His father
was standing with his back to them. Tucking a
quick finger beneath her chin, he spoke intimately, "Don't be coy, Valisa. It does not
become you. It's the new decorating designs—
the ones we decided to have live models for?"

Jason's words carried a question that required
a nod. Bliss, however, had heard nothing of
such plans.

In a husky whisper, Jason said urgently, "We have certain specific persons in mind—*after* the buying trip, and that's where you and I come in."

The models or the buying trip? And what was this all about?

"I don't understand—"

"Play it hard to get, my sweet! Too bad most women never master the game." Then, giving her a sly, suggestive wink, Jason added, "If you and I make the right contacts for him on the trip—all business, on the surface. Well, you're in as the model he has in mind. And I, of course, will be your consort—worth our while in every way—"

A movement of the portfolios on Bliss's desk alerted her to the presence of another person in the room.

Again, as if in replay, Lili Ann had entered. Bliss tried to keep her composure, hoping that the inner flush of guilt she felt did not reflect in her face.

Jason, obviously shaken, hurried in to join his father. Bliss turned to the other girl whose nostrils were flanged with open fury.

"Yes, Lili?"

"I heard that conversation!" Lili Ann hissed.

"I'm sure you did."

"And don't be so complacent. I can ruin you—"

The ringing of the buzzer on her desk saved

Bliss from further encounter. Gratefully, she picked up the portfolios and hurried in to join the two men.

But she felt Lili Ann's anger hot on her back and burning through the door even as it closed behind her. A cold chill of apprehension crept up and down her spine.

There had been a threat—a very real one— in the girl's voice. She was sure to make trouble. Only one course of action was possible now.

I must stop stalling. It is urgent that the game be brought to a climax . . .

As if in a dream, Bliss went through the motions of appearing surprised and overjoyed at Mr. Blackwell's announcement of his plans.

Of course, she would be happy to go. What girl in her right mind would not be?

Yes, she felt confident . . . yes, Mr. Blackwell, sir . . . yes, Jason, I can have other things in order. One week from today will be fine.

And, although she saw the two men through a fog which made their eyes look hollow and their faces appear sunken, she must have made the proper responses.

Mr. Blackwell was shaking her hand in his gentle manner and Jason had moved over to stand beside her on the side opposite his father. There, he pushed closer to her body than was necessary, letting his hand touch her thigh.

Quickly, Bliss checked her watch.

"Oh, thank you both so much," she managed, moving quickly away from Jason. "And now if I can come down from the clouds, I must get to my desk. There must have been a dozen calls!"

Back in her office, Bliss felt a wave of panic sweep over her. She was in over her head. She had become obsessed with this game. It had become a way of life.

Was this, she wondered dully, *how one became addicted to things? Did it have to be alcohol or drugs? Couldn't it be — well, other things as well?*

Leaving a message with her secretary, she left early. But that night she was unable to pray — even for Matt. She felt totally alone. Annihilated.

Oh, Matt, Matt, darling! She sobbed into her pillow.

Chapter Fourteen

F our days before the scheduled trip Mr. Blackwell revealed where Bliss would be going with Jason.

"There will be several stopovers in Europe—"

Europe! True, Bliss had heard mention of overseas travel, but she had never dreamed that it was scheduled for now—or that she would be a part of it.

Concentrate. She must concentrate on what Mr. Blackwell was saying. But she had found no sleep the previous night and her appetite had dwindled. All because of the tension she was under. And now this . . . *concentrate . . . I must concentrate!*

"—and I am sure I need not caution you that the two of you must be very discreet—"

"Discreet?" Bliss managed, wondering what Mr. Blackwell meant. Surely, he didn't know about Jason's advances. And he couldn't know about her plan.

But her heart was suffocating her. It was hard to breathe.

"Uh—yes, discreet—" The man seemed to hesitate and then continued, "You will be showing some partial layouts as previews, doing some buying—and you will need to guard the information as a corporate secret. You were aware of the problems we had several months ago?"

"No—no, I was not."

Bliss wondered if her voice sounded as far away to him as it did to her. The firm's problems had nothing to do with her. But Europe! Europe with Jason! The unthinkable had happened.

Oh, how was she going to handle this? It was all a terrible nightmare—one from which she could not awake.

"Are you all right, Valisa?"

Bliss realized then that Mr. Blackwell was looking at her with concern.

"Oh, yes—just overwhelmed, I guess."

He smiled vaguely.

"Of course—of course. I suggest that you take the remainder of the day off."

Murmuring appreciation, Bliss returned to her

office, did the minimum, then left hurriedly. Fortunately, she did not encounter Jason or Lili Ann.

Back in the apartment, Bliss looked around at what seemed like unfamiliar surroundings. Noonday sunlight slipped through the venetian blinds to cast lozenges of burning bars across the carpet. The room was stale and stifling. And she was short of breath, painfully closed in by walls that were about to crumble.

She had reached her limits, having become enclosed by unexpected barriers. Dry-eyed, she allowed herself to crumple in a shapeless wad on the bed, hoping for the balm of tears.

But tears would not come.

Later Bliss wondered if she dozed. Or was the scene real? Or a frightening figment of her overworked imagination?

It began with the fantasy and nothing had changed—at first. The horse, the rider, and her beautiful self. . .and, then, for the first time, the dream changed. For a split second, the man's face was visible. And it was not Jason's at all. . .somebody quite different. . .a stranger.

Bliss tried to rouse herself, to recognize the face, and then end the fantasy. But, powerless, she could only watch the beautiful dream dissolve, become a swirl of paint-pot colors, and fade into the haunting nightmare.

She was riding away, her body hunched over in despair, her hair sweeping down to cover the face she knew to be disfigured. But something went wrong! Something which brought Bliss to her feet, wet with perspiration from the memory, her mind unable to accept what it had seen.

"It wasn't I at all," she whispered, "and the birthmark wasn't there—just sadness and despair. Who—?"

But before she could phrase the question, the missing fragment came back. A beautiful, youthful face which was at the same time familiar and unfamiliar.

Her grandmother . . . yes, it had to be . . . no, it was Madame Francois . . . then the two faces merged to become one.

Bliss stood transfixed.

" 'Young men shall see visions,' " Matt had quoted. "Wait till I tell him I've seen one!" she whispered to herself. For there was no doubt that a revelation had opened up before her.

Love comes to those with an open heart and, if rejected, will turn away. Love swept through the soul to purify or to destroy, but its silken wings would not flutter in the heart forever. It could be crushed by ugliness from within or without . . . to leave its possessor searching . . . not locked out but locked in . . . forever.

Forever unless one awakened in time! And she had. Oh, she had!

Bliss saw the room come back into focus and for the first time in weeks her mind was clear. Just what she could do had to be decided. Surely there would be a way. It was not too late.

Feeling immeasurably refreshed, Bliss was about to open the blinds and look out at the incoming tide. The sight of the little waves, pulled in and let go by the force of the moon, had always calmed her—given her a clear thinking head. But she had no sooner taken the pull cord than there was a rap at the door.

"Special delivery for Miss McVay."

Even as she signed for the letter, Bliss knew it was from Matt and that it would be postmarked in New York. Her heart sang with joy as she tipped the messenger and tore open the envelope.

But before she sat down to read the contents, Bliss raised her closed eyes to say as if sharing a private joke, "*You* knew all along this would happen, didn't You?"

Then before she burst with joy, she began to read:

My darling Bliss: First I must ask your forgiveness and then your understanding. I was wrong in what I did which only goes to show you that it is not a man without sin who is offering you his heart. In fact, I have little to offer you—nothing, that is but love...

Pressing the letter to her heart, Bliss let her tears flow, welcoming the relief they brought. She felt cleansed. Happy. Reborn!

"He has nothing to give me but love, just *love!* Oh, my darling Matt, it's all I ever wanted—all my life—just love! Even the birthmark wouldn't have bothered me if I had felt loved. Oh, can't you see what the two of you have done for me—you and God?"

She read on then as the shadows gathered, not so much as interrupting herself to turn on a light.

Matt had never left New York. He had always "been in touch, just a heartbeat away... through their mutual loved ones...did Bliss know that Dr. Teegarten was his father's cousin and that was the reason for seeking his advice? Cousin Cedric wanted to invest in the making of the first film...(Bliss wiped her eyes—this was all too much!)...and that he and Francois were reassessing their lives?

Bliss skimmed the words quickly, knowing that she would read the letter time and time again. But what concerned her was Matt's leg, the decision, what could be done.

When she came to that section, Bliss read carefully, then stared at the words incredulously, her heart threatening to break at first and then to burst with joy as its sweetness broke through the numbness the news brought!

When first Cedric told me, I was done in completely. Unable to face it alone. And unable to burden you with the problems with the leg. You have a right to a whole man— not a cripple (yes, amputation was a very real possibility) or one who was terminally ill. . .

There Bliss had to stop and reread.

Amputation. Terminal illness. With all her dark imaginings, those possibilities had never occurred to her. It was hard to read on. Each word could spell an end to the only beautiful thing she had known in life—Matt, their love, and her dreams of togetherness for the future.

Her tear-blurred eyes refused to focus on the letter, seeing instead the vision of Matt's warm, brilliant smile that could make a man handsome even if he were not.

But Matt was! Handsome of features and handsome of heart. So gentle and kind, unlike all other men in the world. Oh, such a beautiful marriage she dreamed of, a perpetual love affair . . . he was so gentle to her. . . gentle the way he would be with their children. . .

With an effort, she pulled herself back to the letter:

I had to threaten the good doctor's life to keep him quiet, but he admitted I had a point and gave me a stay of execution. Advised me to follow the Arabs' way of dealing with the storm. When there's a sandstorm on the desert, you know, they survive by simply pulling their tents over their heads until the storm has passed. Then they get on with their journey. Wise man, my cousin! He knew the Lord wouldn't allow me to hide my head too long...

So Matthew went back, he said, their paths missing each other by his design. Until the diagnosis.

One terrible moment when it appeared that there were cancer cells in the biopsy... another when there was doubt if the muscles and bone could be repaired sufficiently... and would Mr. Thorson sign a release form in case the leg had to be removed?

But, praise the Lord, all had gone well...

Bliss's heart skipped a beat, then did a double beat. It was over. Matt's surgery was over. And Dr. Teegarten's recommended doctors had saved the leg and he, himself, had done the skin grafting. It was over!

Unable to read further, she danced round and round the room, until, overcome with dizziness she fell onto the bed. Laughing. Weeping. And praying all the while. God would understand...

•   •   •

Shortly before she was ready to leave for the office the next morning, Matt's dainty nosegay of white violets arrived to add to her joy.

Bliss had intended to reread his letter, particularly the last paragraph which last night's excitement had interrupted. But when the fragrant flowers came, she used the time to change from the white blouse to a pink-bisque one which would offer a nicer contrast to the white innocence of the violets. Their presence on her shoulder added to her feeling of inner peace.

During the night she had reached a decision. She would tell Mr. Blackwell that she was unable to take the trip after all. Just how much more she would discuss, how deeply she would delve into the past—if she did—would depend on his reaction.

The Lord would guide her, she thought with more self-confidence than the beauty makeover had given her. Confidently, she hurried out.

And just as confidently, she lifted her hand to rap on Mr. Blackwell's door. A movement behind her stopped a follow-through.

Even before turning, Bliss felt that it was Lili Ann who had entered, with her usual uncanny sense of timing.

"I wouldn't do that!" The down-home sweetness was gone from the other girl's voice. It occurred to Bliss for the first time that Lili Ann Paget was not the sweetly helpless creature she appeared to be.

She was a schemer, a clever one, who had

never lived or even visited in Tennessee.

"I'm sorry, Lili," Bliss managed to say politely. "It is necessary that I speak with my employer. Whatever you've come for must wait."

The other girl moved toward her with fluid grace, her eyes glazed with so much hatred that it was frightening.

"Nothing you have to say to the old man in there compares to what I have come to say."

"If it concerns Jason—"

"It concerns you!"

What could Lili Ann possibly have to say to her about herself? She was behaving melodramatically.

Why then did cold fear grip Bliss's heart? Something warned her to be careful. Turning, she motioned Lili Ann to sit down.

"What I have to say can be said standing. It's *you* who had better sit down! How many do you think are fooled?"

"Fooled?"

Shallow breathing made it impossible to say more. How had this girl found out and who else—

"You've managed to blind Jason with your shallow game, but don't you think *I* am onto you? The leak in corporate secrets came the very day the former secretary left—and you're up to the same tricks!"

The truth swept over Bliss then. As Bliss McVay, she was accused of taking the interior decorating designs with her and sharing, selling, or disposing of them in some other self-serving manner.

And truly, there was circumstantial evidence against her. The sudden departure . . . refusal to let her whereabouts be known . . . resigning . . .

"Ah, yes, I have hit a nerve, haven't I, Valisa? Now, do you cancel out at once and recommend me as your replacement or—"

The hissing voice stopped, the silence more significant than an additional flow of words would have been. Bliss felt numbed from head to foot.

The exposure about her real identity had not come. Neither could she reveal it—else she would be accused of what could have all but broken the company.

Why hadn't she thought of something like this? Several clues had been here all along; but, enclosed in her own problem-world, she had failed to interpret them.

"Just what is it that you suspect me of? I fail to see the connection," Bliss said through frozen lips.

Lili Ann's laugh was a sneer.

"Do you think I'm that dumb? That I haven't seen what was going on between the two of you? From the moment you came you've been

giving Jason the inviting glances that landed you
the assignment! And you *know* what he has in
mind. He'll be taking the layouts and the two
of you will be a part of the scam—not that I care
about this firm, mind you! But I warned you that
you were to keep hands off Jason. He's mine!"

Mr. Blackwell's door opened suddenly.

"Ah, good morning, lovely ladies," he said
kindly. "Will you come in now, Valisa? There
are some—uh—details—"

Woodenly, she followed him, listening to his
voice without hearing the words. And just as
woodenly she took her leave. There was no
avenue of escape for right now.

But *why, why,* WHY hadn't God offered a
way of escape when trouble came? But, of
course, she had no right to think His grace would
include her. How could she have expected to
try bargaining with the Creator? Asking forgiveness in advance indeed . . . surely, His Word did
not include that. . . .

•   •   •

In bed that night, Bliss pulled the comforter
up and over her head pretending it was a tent.
But a storm like this would not pass over. It was
one which spawned from wrongdoing, breaking of rules, and she must pay. But how?

The Bible had been her touchstone at a time
when she needed it during the recent times

when she was both troubled and hopeful. Her inspiration when she was grounded. Overburdened with life and its problems. And it had been her link with Matt, who made her feel so complete.

But now she felt completely detached. A part of neither world. A nothing.

Before the storm of tears which left her exhausted, Bliss remembered thinking that the fantasies had reversed momentarily, letting her taste of Eden, then banishing her . . . allowing her to find the promise of fulfillment when she met Matt, reentry into the Garden.

And she had thought the nightmares to be over. But now the ugliness was back. She was rejected . . . oh, what was she going to do?

"Out of the depths have I cried unto thee, O Lord." Exhausted, she slept.

Sleep brought no restoration. Numbly, she dressed for work, realizing that for the first time she could recall she was wearing the same clothing she had worn the day before. The white violets, their petals wilted and their fragrance gone, were still intact.

Vaguely, Bliss tried to remember if there had been a florist's card with the nosegay . . . and where was Matt's letter?

In her excitement, she had forgotten to look for a return address. Maybe, she thought suddenly, there was even a telephone number where she could reach Matt. With the thought, she dug into the pockets of the jacket. Nothing.

The Bible? The letter was not there. Almost in desperation, Bliss clawed into all drawers, checked all shelves, and emptied the contents of her handbag. But the letter was not to be found.

Undoubtedly, it had fallen into the waste basket and the cleaning lady had emptied it.

Sick at heart, she realized that there would be a part of the message she would never read. In her excitement, she had read and committed to memory the loving words, skimming over some of the remainder, and leaving the last paragraph about future plans unread. There was no escape.

"Oh, Lord, I don't ask that You ignore what I have done. Just give the answer for this day and somehow I will make atonement. I won't say 'Amen' because You can expect to hear this over and over. Without You I am nothing, just a fallen sparrow that somehow Your Eye missed."

With the prayer in her heart, Bliss hurried to work, realizing she was going to be late. Traffic crawled. And her nerves were on edge by the time she entered her office. For the first time that Bliss could remember Jason was there before her.

And in her office!

Feeling herself recoil, Bliss whispered, "What are you doing here?"

Jason pulled himself up lazily.

" 'And what are you doing in my chair?' Now, I ask you, is that any way to greet your mate? That's how they will feature us, you know, as man and wife in the illustrations."

"Jason, please, not now—"

But, of course, he misconstrued her meaning.

"The countdown continues for you, too? Only three days. Yes—*maybe* we can wait!"

"There is something I must tell you—"

"I love that intimate whisper of yours." He frowned slightly. "It seems familiar, like your eyes, as if we had been together before—"

The numbness inside Bliss gave way to a flutter of her heart. And then a dangerous swirling of the office furniture around her.

Did he mean . . . did he recognize . . . ?

"But, no, except in my dreams. So it will be a first time together—*alone,* which makes it more exciting!"

Mr. Blackwell saved the moment by opening the entrance door to the joint offices. Bliss had thought the older man was in his private office. He was always early. The thought that she had been alone with Jason further unnerved her.

But there was little time to think of herself because her practiced eye scanned Mr. Blackwell's face and saw that he was ill. The cheeks, usually fresh-shaven and pink, were drawn and the taut skin was more ashen than the graying temples which Bliss thought so distinguishing.

Immediately, she was at his side.

"Mr. Blackwell, here—sit down in my chair. Jason, get your father some water, will you please? Has something happened or—"

He sank into the nearest chair and looked over Bliss's head at a circular weaving on the wall. His eyes traveled the circumferences of the repeated colors as if he were trying to make some sense of the endless design.

Refusing the water Jason offered, Mr. Blackwell, with his eyes still trying to focus on the weaving, said, "Gone—all gone—it's going to be like the other time."

"Mr. Blackwell—" Bliss began.

But Jason interrupted.

"I will take care of this. It's all right, Father. The firm will survive. This trip will more than make up the losses we suffered before—"

This time it was Mr. Blackwell who interrupted.

"But you never told me how great the losses were—or who took the layouts—and now some more are missing—".

Jason seemed to be breathing hard. And yet there was no sign of concern for his father. Something was wrong here. Something Jason was keeping from his father.

"We never knew, Father. And we didn't want to bother you during the illness. It's plain to see you've been overworking—here, I'm going to take you home. Valisa and I can manage with Lili's help."

"Gone—all gone—" Mr. Blackwell repeated. "And I never knew until I saw the books this morning—gone—"

His dark face filled with something akin to fear, Jason managed to move his father quickly into his office before Bliss could be of assistance. Moments later, she heard the door of the outer office close.

Bliss tried to concentrate. The layouts needed hours more work. In her mind she could see the rooms, perfect in their abstractness. A *home*, with loving wooden arms to enfold a shadow family, babies with dandelion curls! Her. . .Matt. . .

How could she go so far afield? Imagine her and Matt together when there was such a gathering storm here? Maybe Lili Ann had heard from Jason. Why hadn't he called?

But the other girl had gone home, a note said, because she felt one of her migraines coming on.

In desperation, Bliss realized that this meant night work. Here with Jason. *Alone*. . . .

Chapter Fifteen

❧

*A*n empty office is like an off-season carousel, Bliss thought, *so lifeless, so* tomb-quiet. But even as the comparison came to mind, it was disturbing. Too like the horses of her daydreams and nightmares. . . other-worldly steeds, open-mouthed in their speed. . . and then the silences.

As the lights of the city went on to sparkle across the bay, Bliss tried to calm her jangled nerves by looking at the spectacle below. Surely it would soothe her as it always did.

But the growing sense of fear and apprehension persisted. With shaking fingers, she telephoned for a sandwich and coffee to be sent up and redoubled her efforts to achieve the "yin and yang," that Mr. Blackwell insisted upon.

"Decorating," the talented man said repeatedly, "must be in perfect balance."

Yes, like life. . . then, forcing her mind back to the layout in front of her, Bliss renewed her efforts.

Mr. Blackwell was right. These *had* to be finished tonight. Then tomorrow she would resign . . .

Engrossed in the intricate details of a European-flavored home, Bliss became lost in her work. The scene came to life beneath her paintbrush—every detail including the sophisticated hosts and their guests, all in evening wear . . . butlers gliding by laden with crystal glasses . . . perfect, just perfect for the Designer's Show. Movable wall, spiral wrought-iron staircase . . . *sweet opiate of work!*

In that state of near-euphoria, Bliss was unaware that someone had entered the room until one light went out and then two. Maybe her eyes were just tired.

What time was it anyway? She had been in a state of near-hysteria and the work had been like a massive shot of some unknown tranquilizer. Realizing that her back was aching with fatigue, she stood, stretched, and blinked her eyes to clear her vision.

"Beautiful! Do that again for me, Valisa."

Jason's voice cut across the stillness, both startling and angering Bliss.

Where had he been when she needed him? And what was his purpose in coming in as if on padded paws? Then both emotions gave way to fear as she heard the deadbolt slip into place.

What on earth did he think he was doing? And why was he lurking in the shadows and switching off lights as thieves did in some second-rate movie?

To bolster her own courage, Bliss managed to say, "Where have you been, Jason? I've waited so long." She hated herself that the words came out as a whisper.

Before answering, Jason flipped another switch. The room was filled with intimate shadows. And Bliss's heart was filled with terror.

But she managed to say, "Stop being dramatic, Jason—we've no time to waste—"

Jason, his dark features made darker by the shadows, emerged from behind a clump of potted ferns.

"I love it when you whisper like that, Valisa. And I love it when you sound eager! It's the sweetest music there is to man's ear to hear a woman *urge* him!"

Bliss was paralyzed and unable to move, the way she had felt in the nightmare.

Get me through this, Lord, I beg—whatever Your price, her heart cried out. Aloud she said,

"I'm not urging, Jason. I'm ordering. And I resent your insinuations!"

Step-by-step he came menacingly closer, his arms outstretched, his laugh unpleasant to hear.

"Come, my sweet! Isn't it time you stopped the handkerchief dropping?"

There was no denial in Bliss's voice, just pleading.

"Jason, you don't understand—and I've tried to find a way to tell you! Listen to me now. Please listen! There's been a terrible misunderstanding. I—I'm not who you think—or what you think—"

But his arms were around her, smothering her, shutting off her breath. Struggle as she would, there was no way to free herself. Her struggling seemed only to intrigue him, cause him to tighten his grip, dig into the flesh of her shoulders, and laugh triumphantly.

It was an ugly sound. The laugh of a man possessed. A madman!

"Please—" Bliss tried to whisper.

But his mouth came down on hers in a bruising kiss. Even as she fought against Jason, some faraway part of her was thinking wildly that this had nothing to do with love. It was raw passion. The kind that made her feel unclean. Ashamed to be a woman.

Oh, how could she have thought that this man, once aroused, would propose anything so honorable as marriage? And how could she have been so blind, so foolish, so *vain* as to want him on any terms?

Was this God's way of imposing penance? No, no, God couldn't be so cruel. . .He was a God of love. . .*Lord, help me!* her heart cried out.

In a last burst of energy, Bliss managed to turn her face aside and scream. When Jason laughed drunkenly she realized how futile it was. Everybody had gone home hours ago. The door was bolted. And, even should the cleaning crew come to this wing of the offices, Jason would have hung a WORKING—DO NOT DISTURB sign on the doorknob.

There had to be another way! Drawing her hand up with a strength that surprised her, Bliss clawed at thin air helplessly.

Then Jason made the mistake of forcing his lips against her mouth in another crazed kiss. Bliss brought the free hand up then and with all her might drew her nails across his face, sickened at the furrows she felt them dig in his flesh.

With a scream of pain and anger, Jason released his grip; and Bliss ran wildly toward the door. No, there would be no escape, for— although she could release the deadbolt from the inside—he would have turned the key in the lock below and pocketed the key.

The window! How far was it to the fire escape?

Stumbling against furniture in the darkness, Bliss rushed toward the window she knew opened and felt for the lock in the darkness. The window slid open soundlessly at the touch of her hand and for a moment there was hope.

The flicker died instantly. There was no way she could reach the fire escape from here as it connected with Jason's office and she would have to cross the room. . . still it was worth a try. . . where was he?

But before she was able to so much as turn, she was imprisoned by his hard, angry arms. His breath was hot on her face and she realized for the first time that it reeked of alcohol. Again, the struggle—more furious this time.

He's killing me, she remembered thinking as she fought for her life. She could taste blood in her mouth. Her clothes were being ripped to shreds. And he was dragging her bodily toward the sectional couch. . .

This couldn't be happening. . . it was part of the nightmare. . .

But the thud on the office floor had to be real as a swinging figure landed lightly on his feet and bounded toward where she was struggling with Jason.

Bliss, having used up all the adrenalin her body could manufacture, was unable to move. She should be helping this superman, whoever he was. . . calling the police. . . *something.*

But frozen in shock, she could only watch the exchange of blows, hear Jason's curses, and wonder why the other man had not spoken. Vaguely, she wondered about his identity and how he could have climbed to the window when the private balconies were separated widely by a narrow ledge that encircled the building.

And then it was all too much. Her head was filled with helium. It was floating away. Leaving her body. A body that had grown too limp to stand erect any longer. Aware that the struggle was still going on and that there were stabbing pains throughout her body, Bliss sank to the floor.

Then merciful darkness engulfed her.

• • •

Behind closed eyelids, Bliss felt the searing red circles give way to smaller pink ones. Then the colored mists cleared and she was aware of motion. Gentle rocking. They were on a plane, that was it! She and Matt were high above the clouds. She was in his arms. And he was soothing her as one soothes a child.

"Easy does it, darling. Just lie still. You will be all right now. I arrived just in time—"

And then it all came back.

Jason! Where was he? She must escape! Wildly, she tried to reach out only to have a pair of gentle hands take hers.

"Easy, darling—you're home."

Matt. It *was* Matt! This couldn't be a dream. Her eyes flew open and she was looking into his beautiful face. Such relief and love spread over her being that Bliss wanted to sing for joy. And instead she could only break into a childish whimper.

"Oh, Matt," she murmured anticlimactically, "I must look a fright—"

"You look beautiful," he whispered against her ear. "Now, lie there relaxed and tell me all about it. Then we will take care of those scratches—and a lot of other things."

"I will, oh, I will—tell you everything, I mean. But, oh, Matt, how did you find me? How on earth *could* you have scaled that wall? And—"

Matt laughed softly.

"Whoa! One question at a time. You forget I'm a stuntman. Now, let's hear the story—*every* word or I'll twist your ear!"

Unnerved as Bliss was from the nightmarish episode in her office and fatigued as she was from the strain of recent weeks, she relaxed completely in Matt's arms. Nothing else mattered now. Nothing else in this world.

Yes, she would bare her soul. Hide nothing. But first there were some questions she must ask.

"Matt, how *could* you have known which office I was in—"

"You screamed, remember?"

Yes, she remembered. But how had he known where she was . . . and why didn't he tell her he was coming?

"I had the address of the office and guessed you were there when you did not answer the apartment phone or the bell. And I *did* tell you I was coming to you, my darling, in the letter's last paragraph—just as soon as my leg permitted."

The last paragraph . . . the one she had not read . . . but none of that mattered. With a start, she tried to sit up. How could she have forgotten anything so important as Matt's surgery?

"Oh, Matt—I'm sorry—your leg—"

Gently, he pushed her back down into his arms. But not before she saw a heavy cast beneath the tweed trousers.

"Good weapon, you know. The old 'punt' kick works every time—"

"Jason! You and Jason fought. Are you all right?" When she tried again to rise, once again Matt pushed her back into the cradle of his arms. So much to ask. But not now.

They talked until dawn. The east window drapes turned pink with the promise of sunrise, but something magical had happened. Everything was poured out between them. *Everything!* And there had been no recriminations. No look of disappointment. Just understanding and love.

To Bliss's surprise, Matt knew almost all of the story anyway. But how?

"Through Madame Francois. You made quite a hit there," he chuckled. "She fancies herself the mediary to communicate between you and your grandmother—"

"Oh, Matt, you don't entertain such ideas— or think that I do!" Bliss said in disbelief.

Matt held her closer.

"Of course not, but we can't take away another's conviction without offering a better substitute. I told her that Jesus is my intercessor between God and me."

Something warm and comforting closed around Bliss's heart.

"Is that really how it works?"

"That's how it works."

Seeming to sense the peace that was stealing over her, Matt drew her closer. She could feel the steady beating of his heart. "Be-lieve. . . be-lieve." it seemed to throb.

But if one gave in whole-heartedly that surrender meant rules carved out in stone. Rules she had violated.

Frightened, Bliss turned the question on Madame Francois.

"Didn't she violate a rule—contacting you— giving information about a client?"

"Yes," Matt said slowly and carefully, "I suppose she did. But she took it upon herself to

choose the right man for you. Isn't love worth
a risk, my darling?"

Bliss felt the familiar tingle along her spine.
Love? Love was worth everything. *Everything*.

"Yes, even the risks," Matt continued.

"Is she—afraid?"

"Afraid? Madame Francois? Not now. Not
with Cousin Cedric and me lined up against her.
I left her reading *The Book of Psalms* I gave her.
Nothing more. The finding of one's faith is a
delicate thing."

*Oh, wonderful, wonderful Matt, how proud
God must be of you . . . leading us all so gently
. . . letting us discover . . .*

The drapes had deepened from pink to rose.
Soon the sun would chin itself in the east, toss
a handful of brilliant gems on the incoming tide,
and get on with the day . . .

As she must get on with hers! But first there
was a question she must ask. A crucial one.
Then she could face the day with the knowledge
that she did not need an Arab's tent. God would
have offered her His wings instead and she could
ride out the storm that lay ahead.

"Jason," she whispered, "tell me if God's going to forgive me for breaking all His rules? There
are so many I never can live up to."

Lips against her hair, Matt said with quiet conviction, "None of us can, Bliss. That's why He
sent His Son. Just keep one rule in mind—

His new commandment, which is love!"

Did she or did she not hear the soft whirring and feel herself and Matt drawn closer together by a Force stronger even than the love they felt for one another?

Forever after, she would remember the moment of deep peace and overwhelming love as the touch-of-the-wings turn in her life. All doubts dissolved. And, in her state of exhilaration, there was no fatigue or pain left in her body.

How beautiful to meet God in Person. . .

Reluctantly, she pulled away from the circle of Matt's arms.

"Nothing slept but both my feet and yet I feel wonderful!"

And just as reluctantly he let her go.

"So do I, my darling—and yet we both know what you must do, don't we?"

"Yes, Matt, we both know."

"I'm ordering breakfast sent up for us here while you shower and dress your prettiest. What you have to do won't be easy. But you'll be yourself. No more acting, ever, except in my movies. Promise?"

"I promise" she called happily as she limped toward the bathroom. "And by the way, you'll have to marry me, you know—having spent the night here."

Matt made a mock grimace and picked up the telephone.

Chapter Sixteen

raffic was lighter than usual as Bliss crossed the Bay Bridge. Or maybe she simply took no notice in her complete happiness. Sailboats were out already. What a perfect day for sailing away into Never-Never Land. . .only she had found it.

"And I have You to thank," she murmured aloud, glancing upward at the faultless sky. "And I will keep Your commandment of love, Lord. Oh, I can do that! I know Your love will get me through this day. . ."

Should she drive? Matt had wondered. Bliss had assured him that she should. But now she wondered if anyone as happy as she was a good risk! She wanted to shout. She wanted to sing. She wanted to live forever. And she would. God had even seen to that!

And Matt had taken care of the rest. As she made the last turn leading to Blackwell & Son's, Bliss looked back on his binding up her wounds and her heart so that the injuries did not show. He had managed to make her laugh at his reference to their combined experience with plastic surgery, which, he said, gave him the license to apply Band-Aids of see-through plastic.

Then, assuring her of his undying love while holding her breathlessly close, he had blotted out last night's horrible nightmare completely.

In a crisp linen suit with becoming wide lapels, her face, nails, and hair perfectly groomed, she stepped confidently into her office. She was about to buzz Mr. Blackwell's office when the white violets arrived.

Deliberately taking time to pin them on her shoulder, Bliss planned her first move. She would walk through the rest on the legs of faith. With new strength, she picked up the phone.

"Good morning, Mr. Blackwell! This is Bliss McVay."

"Good morning, Miss McVay. And won't you come in, please? I was expecting your call."

When in a matter of moments later Bliss stood before him, there was no surprise in her employer's face. Just sadness. No, more. *Heart-break*. How much he knew and how he knew it was a mystery. But she knew a broken heart when she saw it. All her life until recently one had met her eyes each time she looked into a mirror.

"Miss McVay . . . Mr. Blackwell," they spoke simultaneously. And simultaneously they laughed.

"Be seated," he said kindly. "I want you to know that I am aware of last night's dreadful incident. I apologize for him, but Jason will be asking forgiveness in person shortly. I have invited the top executives to join us—"

"Oh, no—there are things I must tell you—"

Mr. Blackwell went on as if there had been no interruption, ". . . *after* you and I have talked. Now, what is it that you would like to tell me, my dear?"

Bliss raised remorseful eyes to Mr. Blackwell's face.

"I want you to know how sorry I am about all this—this deception—"

A smile played at the corners of his mouth.

"Quite clever, I would say. Deception? No, I would prefer to call it *masquerade.*"

How kind he was. But there was so much to clear up. Apologies. Explanations. And then she herself must be cleared of the ugly accusations . . .

"How long have you known?" Bliss whispered, the conversation having taken such a surprising turn that she was uncertain how to handle it all.

Mr. Blackwell's level gaze met her own. Open. Honest. And, Bliss realized suddenly, the dark eyes were more clear and his thinking more lucid than on previous days.

"I have known since the beginning, which is to say from the time you left. You see, painful as it is for an aging father to say this about his son—well, this is not a first offense—or affair. It was not you but my son of whom I was suspicious. That is why I had you followed—"

"Followed?"

"Day by day. So you were no stranger applying for this job. Neither was it by accident that you ended up in my office. You are guilty of nothing."

"But the layouts which are missing—and the money they lost the firm—I realize that I must look bad in your eyes." She raised stricken eyes to his and saw only kindness.

Bliss realized that tears had come in spite of her morning resolve. Perhaps if things had been difficult, she could have remained poised. But to be reassured that she was innocent after all her fears and cheap tricks was just too much.

"But you don't understand, sir. I wanted to be beautiful for your son. Once I fancied myself in love with him—and I sought beauty for the wrong reason—"

"Well, then, let us say that the boy did one noble thing! What makes you think you have no right to beauty? Now, about the money— you are not a suspect. But," he added helplessly, "I must confess that we cannot account for the disappearance of the layouts."

When the buzzer on his desk sounded, Mr. Blackwell said kindly, "Dry your eyes so they won't accuse me of beating helpless women in my senility. And rest assured that nobody knows of your masquerade except the two of us, as far as I know. I have not revealed it."

The employees Mr. Blackwell had summoned came in uncertainly. Aware that something unusual was about to take place, they sat down. There was no effort at conversation. Although her insides churned with apprehension, Bliss forced herself to appear poised, greeting each of the personnel with a smile or nod of her head. Praying for strength, she forced her eyes to Jason's face.

But he avoided her eyes. His face, eyes averted, was pale so that the scratches stood out, red and angry. But something about his body language was even more revealing. The usual erectness which so distinguished him was gone. Slumped in defeat. Almost unrecognizable. And his hands were fumbling with a rubber band, twisting it back and forth nervously. This man who was always so sure of himself. So arrogant. So in command . . .

About to turn back to Mr. Blackwell, Bliss was suddenly aware of a pair of burning eyes fixed on her.

She felt rather than saw the hatred even before meeting the narrowed gaze of Lili Ann, whose face had been hidden behind the man seated in front of her. Then the expression changed. Changed so suddenly that Bliss was caught off guard.

Why, the girl was gloating, actually *gloating*. But why—

Mr. Blackwell interrupted her thoughts with a delicate clearing of his throat. Then he stood, a tall, imposing man in complete charge of himself and the situation. Fleetingly, Bliss saw him as a judge who was about to pronounce sentence—then as a lawyer about to read a last will and testament to white-faced relatives who knew they had not been named heirs. Then her mind cleared as he began.

"What I have to say will not take long, important to the firm as it is. There are several personnel changes I wish to make and I would appreciate having those of you with questions to see me privately." He glanced at his watch and then continued, "I have an appointment following this meeting."

Whatever Bliss had expected, it was not this. And the others sat frozen to their chairs in a manner that said they, too, were puzzled, surprised, and afraid.

"As you know, there was a great loss recently —one which we dare not have recur. Consequently, my son will be moving into the shipping room—beginning at the bottom to study the business, providing he wishes to remain."

There was the sound of intaken breath. And the groan of disbelief must have been from Jason. As if watching a movie, Bliss felt herself strain forward wondering what would happen next.

"He will be replaced by my secretary if she wishes—"

There was no time for Bliss to take in the full meaning of what the man had said. Before he could complete his sentence, there was the sound of an overturned chair and a screech which seemed to split the office in half.

Then Lili Ann was in front of Bliss, pointing an accusing finger.

"I warned you, you cheap, undermining schemer! Coming in to usurp us all—our jobs— our men! Well, you'll be sorry!" she screamed in fury. Then, ignoring Mr. Blackwell's uplifted hand, Lili brought herself under control and spoke in honeyed tones, "She's not who she claims. I have proof—"

"I don't need proof, Miss Paget! My secretary is Miss Bliss Valisa LaBelle McVay!" The way he spoke dismissed all charges, giving a little implication that Bliss's identity was something the two of them had planned.

"But she undermined us all—*stole* from the company—"

Something happened inside Bliss then. There was a moment's dizziness, a blurring of her eyes which caused her accuser to disappear completely. Only to reappear in a different setting.

Jason's office . . . of course . . . that was it . . . Lili Ann bringing in papers, rummaging through his files, pretending to need signatures. Her presence there had been more than an attempt to attract him . . . but what?

And then the dizziness cleared. Distinctly in her mind's eye Bliss saw the layouts, remembered seeing the other girl pick them up, pretend not to understand "nasty numbers," only to scribble something in her notebook. And when she left the portfolios were gone.

"It was you all along. You, Lili." Bliss had not known she was going to speak until the words were whispered.

"She lies. She *lies!*" Honeyed tones gone, Lili Ann was out of control. "Ask her to prove it—"

Bliss inhaled deeply. This was regrettable, but it was necessary to get the truth out in the open.

Closing her eyes, she said slowly, "SS-19842-

Z-42, September 15; SS-19843-Z-43, September 16. . .need I go on?"

"No, my dear," Mr. Blackwell said, pressing the button for a computer readout of the dates. . .

Bliss would never remember the rest of the meeting. Exhaustion had taken its toll and she was only vaguely aware of Mr. Blackwell's saying, ". . .Complete retribution or a full report to authorities". . .an apology to Miss McVay was in order from both Lili Ann and Jason. . .and did Miss McVay wish to press charges?

No, she must forgive. . .

Then, to her relief, it was over. Mr. Blackwell said the matters were not open for discussion and dismissed the group with a promise that a totally new start was in the offing. At last, blessedly, they were gone.

But she was frozen to her chair. Or had Mr. Blackwell asked her to stay? He must have for, with a smile, he said, "I will send for our visitor now." And before there was time to inquire if she should leave, he buzzed the receptionist.

Then Matt was there. *Matt!* But how. . .why. . .what? Her trembling hand went automatically to her heart and then to her face. Her face. . .the face she and Matt had not even discussed, she found herself thinking foolishly. They had been too involved. . .too much had happened. . .no, that wasn't it!

Matthew Thorson, beautiful Matt, had loved her for herself—had discovered in her an inner beauty . . .

But what is he doing here? Oh, surely it can't be a dream! Dear God, no dream—please no dream—

But there is no sound in dreams. And the two men were speaking to each other and to her.

"Good to see you again, Thorson," Mr. Blackwell shook hands with Matt. "We met last night—here, just before taking you home. He told me about the film and we did some temporary planning while the doctor examined you—" Mr. Blackwell said to Bliss.

Doctor? Film? Plans?

And then the blood which had seemed to drain from Bliss's body rushed back. Matt had stepped behind her chair and placed one warm hand on her taut shoulder, letting the fingers of the other hand gently lift her hair and massage her neck. The world came back in focus. She relaxed, letting her heart pick up tempo when his touch became a caress. It was hard to listen, but she would try.

"So," the older man was saying, "maybe we can work something out if you would be willing to share Bliss's services with me. Portions of the filming could be done here, giving proper credit. Good advertising for me and a good financial boost for you new business."

Reaching up, she touched Matt's hand. It closed over her own. Mr. Blackwell, watching, must have known he had his answer.

"Shall we draw up a contract?" he smiled.

"Darling?" Matt whispered the question.

With a heart full of love but no voice, Bliss could only nod. Beautiful rooms flashed before her eyes, made to live in, made to love in— with special people in mind.

Oh, there were so many lovely stories to tell about love, *real* love—the holy kind that God Himself plans between a man and his mate. Love such as hers and Matt's. . . Dr. Teegarten and Madame Francois. . . titled, *When Love Shines Through*. . .

"Did you hear that, Bliss?" Matthew's voice was honed with excitement. And she could only shake her head, the head that had been lost in a lover's dream.

"Mr. Blackwell wants us to go ahead with the trip to Europe. Thinks you can handle it. And it would give me a chance to look around, do some filming, make some contacts—"

"And honeymoon!" Mr. Blackwell reminded.

It was incredulous. It was impossible. Bliss and Matt were on the white horse. . . riding through a field of poppies. . . with God's love shining through the clouds to light the entire world. With *Him* all things were possible. . .

Tactfully, Mr. Blackwell left to draw up the

contracts. Bliss raised her bright and luminous face to receive Matt's kiss.

And Madame Francois would have finally said the eyes were right!

Rhapsody Romances

- ☐ **Another Love**, Joan Winmill Brown   3906
- ☐ **The Candy Shoppe**, Dorothy Abel   3884
- ☐ **The Heart That Lingers**, June Masters Bacher   3981
- ☐ **Love's Tender Voyage**, Joan Winmill Brown   3957
- ☐ **Promise Me Forever**, Colette Collins   3973
- ☐ **The Whisper of Love**, Dorothy Abel   3965
- ☐ **If Love Be Ours**, Joan Winmill Brown   4139
- ☐ **One True Love**, Arlene Cook   4163
- ☐ **Reflection of Love**, Susan Feldhake   4201
- ☐ **Until Then**, Dorothy Abel   4171
- ☐ **Until There Was You**, June Masters Bacher   4198
- ☐ **With All My Heart**, June Masters Bacher   4104
- ☐ **Forever Yours**, Arlene Cook   4383
- ☐ **Let Me Love Again**, Joan Winmill Brown   4392
- ☐ **My Heart To Give**, Carmen Leigh   4368
- ☐ **The Tender Melody**, Dorothy Abel   4287
- ☐ **Touched By Diamonds**, Colette Collins   4279
- ☐ **When Love Shines Through**, June Masters Bacher   4309

$2.95 each

At your local bookstore or use this handy coupon for ordering.

HARVEST HOUSE PUBLISHERS

1075 ARROWSMITH, EUGENE, OREGON 97402

Please send me the book(s) I have checked above. I am enclosing $_____ (please add 50¢ per copy to cover postage and handling). Send check or money order—no cash or C.O.Ds. Please allow four weeks for delivery.

Name _____

Address _____

City _____ State _____ Zip _____

Phone _____

Dear Reader:

We would appreciate hearing from you regarding the Rhapsody Romance series. It will enable us to continue to give you the best in inspirational romance fiction.

Mail to: Rhapsody Romance Editors
Harvest House Publishers, 1075 Arrowsmith, Eugene, OR 97402

1. What most influenced you to purchase **WHEN LOVE SHINES THROUGH**?
   - ☐ The Christian Story
   - ☐ Cover
   - ☐ Backcover copy
   - ☐ Recommendations
   - ☐ Other Rhapsody Romances you've read
   - ☐ _____

2. Your overall rating of this book:
   ☐ Excellent ☐ Very good ☐ Good ☐ Fair ☐ Poor

3. Which elements did you find most appealing in this book?
   - ☐ Heroine
   - ☐ Hero
   - ☐ Setting
   - ☐ Story line
   - ☐ Love Scenes
   - ☐ Christian message

4. How many Rhapsody Romances have you read all together? (Choose one) ☐ 1-2 ☐ 3-6 ☐ 7-10 ☐ Over 11

5. How likely would you be to purchase other Rhapsody Romances?
   - ☐ Very likely
   - ☐ Somewhat likely
   - ☐ Not very likely
   - ☐ Not at all

6. Please check the box next to your age group.
   - ☐ Under 18
   - ☐ 18-24
   - ☐ 25-34
   - ☐ 35-39
   - ☐ 50-54
   - ☐ Over 55

Name _____

Address _____

City _____ State _____ Zip _____